This is Helen Bateman's debut nov
Language and Literature at Lancaster
both subjects at Secondary school lev
with her husband and looks after their three children full time.
Writing is something Helen has always enjoyed and she feels
blessed to now have more time to indulge in this privilege.

www.facebook.com/helenbatemanauthor

https://twitter.com/hbatemanauthor

If you like this book please review on Amazon or Goodreads
and share with others using #soultotake

Soul to take

by

Helen Bateman

For all the precious Souls I have loaned including
Harry, Lily and Grace.

For my loving parents, Brenda and Joe,
who have taken care of my Soul for so long.

For my inspirational husband, Andy,
who is the true mate of my Soul.

VICKY

"The world was spinning before I was born and it will spin long after I'm gone. It's so easy to be a Nobody. I need to prove that I was here. To make my mark. To be remembered. To live on."

Vicky tidies away the last sparkling, white plate from the dishwasher, closes the kitchen cupboard, rests her petite, skinny-jeaned bottom against the dark, granite worktop and seems pleased with her statement. She looks over to Dan for approval but there's no sign of any; he merely raises a mug of tea to his lips and continues to flick the pages of his newspaper.

"I've been there two months now and hardly anyone even knows my name yet. I'm just not sure I'm going to get the recognition my skill set deserves," she goes on.

"Look, love," Dan finally replies, folding the paper, "What does any o' that matter? 'ow many people d'y'think are bothered about me at work? Long as I visit me farmers and tell 'em what they want t'hear, everyone's 'appy. An' anyway, if it's recognition you're after, just wait 'til y'come 'ome. Yer gettin' yerself involved in plenty in't village. Ev'ry one loves y' here.

Y'll be the Queen o'Freddock, one day. Stop bein' daft an' get t' yer committee meetin'."

"You're right," she concedes, grabs what looks to be a fur jacket and totters through the hallway, towards the front door.

"That new?" Dan looks on.

"Yep. *New Look* sale. Nineteen, ninety nine," she lies.

She's off, clippety clopping down the High Street, mobile phone in hand, clearing off the last few emails from work. She stops and slows down. I've seen this manoeuvre so many times now. Ten minutes late is just far too early for Vicky. People might think she's got nothing better to do than go to the meeting. She dives into the doorway of the village shop. In a frantic assessment of what she could feasibly be in there to buy, she spies Maggie shopping in the corner.

Although I've noticed Maggie around the village recently, I've not seen Vicky with Maggie before. It would appear they've not seen each other in a while either; their right cheeks are drawn together but they do not meet. The cold, freezer aisle air is kissed by both ladies. In the same moment that Vicky resumes her original upright position, Maggie goes in for the more continental double kiss greeting. There is an awkward fumbling around and a rather theatrical, red lipstick smudge results on Vicky's nose. As

I have learned recently, no-one tells Vicky anything that she doesn't want to hear. The blemish remains.

"Dahhhrrrling, how aaarrrre you?" Maggie asks the entire shop. She is dressed head to toe in azure blue. Her silky dress, which can only have started out its days on the stage, flows from bronzed shoulders right down to the floor. Matching silk gloves and earrings glisten as the two ladies talk. It is hard to put an age on Maggie. She could be forty-something, fifty-something, or beyond. Good old war paint and a mahogany, shoulder length wig hide the secrets of her years. Maggie has clearly made her mark on the world.

"Going anywhere nice?" Vicky asks.

"No, just had a late one at school. The little dahrlings made a dreadful mess of the props cupboard this afternoon. Maybe I should have saved tidying up as the objective for tomorrow's lesson!" Maggie laughs. "I have got a good game with a boxful of old spectacles up my sleeve though. That should keep them occupied for a while," she plans aloud.

I'm not sure what is most surreal: the fact that Maggie has been teaching in the local Primary all day, dressed in her current attire, her casual attitude towards teaching methods or the fact that her arm is weighed down by a basket containing a box of half-price strawberries and a rather withered-looking cucumber.

"*Pimms*," Maggie adds when she realises Vicky is staring at her goods, "Thought I might need a little *Pimms* later. Anyway, you must get off to your meeting. You're doing an amazing job, I hear, Vicky. That committee was nothing before you were Chair. You've turned it around, dahrling."

With that strong emotional pat on the back, Vicky trots over to the cash machine by the door, visibly beaming. Transaction complete, her phone rings.

"Mum! Hi! Fine thanks. Yeah, I've had a great week. Oh, everything about it is better, especially the money. And it looks better on my CV. Dan says it's the best marketing company to work for in Leeds. The journey's not too bad either. How's life in Spain treating you? Que tal? You impressed?"

As the device talks back, the mask momentarily slips. Vicky's tone has changed and only her eyes speak the truth. "Why would we want to move to Leeds? I know it would be nearer to work but Dan's family is just around the corner and quality of life is so much better here. It's so beautiful." There is a pause. "I don't remember saying that about people who lived in villages. There's loads to do. I'm off to a committee meeting right now." The regurgitation of what Dan constantly tells her almost sounds convincing.

Venturing further towards her destination, Vicky surveys the scene around her. It is indeed 'beautiful'. The imposing Thirteenth Century church casts a protective shadow over its garden of those who will never leave. Floodlights showcase the well-manicured village green and the daffodils' yearly cycle is beginning as green shoots optimistically spear through the cold, brown earth. Opposite the church, Freddock Primary School stands central and magnetic. Even in the still of the evening, its reputation pulls wealthy parents from an enormous force field. Those who want something a little better for their precious offspring are drawn here like zombies, casting aside what they previously thought was a sensible amount of money to pay for a three bedroomed semi-detached. I suppose the shenanigans of the Drama Department aren't too widely broadcast. No, there it stands, idyllic and proud, showing that Freddock is the ultimate place to bring up a family.

Vicky finally arrives at the Village Hall. Green paint crumbles from a wooden door which creaks as she opens it. Slightly taken aback as she enters, Vicky's nose makes the most subtle of twitches, the kind a person unconsciously makes in response to an unpleasant odour. It could be the smell of soured milk from the beaker I saw spilt here this morning at Toddler Group or maybe from the damp fur of the yapping cocker spaniel who sat in the 'congregation' of the Pet Service the church held here on Sunday. Nevertheless, Vicky's senses quickly adjust and she makes her entrance. With a beaming smile, she scans the room to be acknowledged. Four blue, plastic tables are arranged in a rectangular formation and the committee are seated at brown plastic chairs. The meeting has not yet started but they are clearly waiting, already informally discussing the issues which have brought them away from their homes on a chilly February evening.

"You've started, then?" Vicky drapes her coat on the back of the only remaining empty chair and sits down. An apology or explanation would ruin the mystique.

"No, no," replies an elderly gentleman, "Just 'aving a chat while we waited for you." I understand the point being made and see the eyebrows begin raised, even if Vicky does not.

"Well," Vicky begins, "I think the main objectives we need to address this evening are marketing of our Summer Fair and health and safety on the actual day of the event."

"Okay," a lady tentatively replies while opening a small pad of paper. "Shall I note that down or wait until you explain it to us?"

"Can I just say, before we get any further," interrupts the elderly gentleman. "An' I want this documented," he points a spindly finger at the notebook, "that there were 'ardly any teabags left in our cupboard when we come in tonight and there was an 'ole box left after last meeting. Someone else's been using 'em and I'm not going to keep paying for 'em if they're going to keep usin' 'em."

"Yes, Norman, I noticed that too."

"Right," Vicky nods to the secretary, "perhaps you could pop that in the 'Any Other Business', Barbara, and we'll discuss it at the end."

"Okay, Vicky," she scribbles, "Can I just say, it's not the Toddler Group Committee taking the teabags; we have a rota system so we never run out and it was my turn last month."

"I'm not throwing 'round accusations, Barbara. I just want it sortin'," Norman retorts.

"So anyway," Vicky looks exasperated already, "I was thinking about marketing of the fair and it occurred to me that most families have kids in Freddock Primary, don't they? So, I wondered if we could put some flyers in the book bags."

"Flyers?" pipes up a previously silent voice from the corner.

"Small pieces of paper with the main details on?"

"Right," he laughs, "I see. We've never done that before."

"Frances, you've got kids in school, haven't you? Would you be able to ask the Headmaster for us?"

"Yes, of course," she obeys.

"You know them teabags," Norman's thoughts have clearly not drifted very far, "I think we need to be asking questions t'Bowling Club. As I say, I'm not going 'round accusin' folk but they're the only ones it can be."

And so the committee meeting continues. For three long hours they mull over Vicky's marketing ideas, the health and safety issues, which as Norman points out have never been a problem for twenty five years, and most importantly, teabags. Finally, Vicky announces, "Lastly, I wondered if anyone would prefer to have the meeting at the pub next time?"

A general mumbling and shaking of heads indicates that a change of venue would be a revolutionary step too far. Vicky's attempt to divert from teabag debates is quashed for another month. As the tables are folded away and the chairs are stacked in neat rows in the corner, Vicky makes a beeline for Barbara and Frances, who are deep in conversation.

"Erm, it's my birthday next Friday and we're having a few drinks at our house. Wondered if you'd like to come?" she interrupts.

"I'll have to check with hubby," says Barbara, "but thanks."

"Bring him too. Get a babysitter. That's great then. See you both about eightish?"

Frances' only option is to nod, smile and watch as Vicky bounces out into the cool evening air.

Victorious in her quest, Vicky returns home. As she opens the front door and walks into the hallway, Dan is putting his coat on to leave, "Just off for a pint wi' John. Back soon. How was the meeting?"

"They're unbelievable, Dan. I spend hours trying to bring Freddock Summer Fair into the Twenty-first Century, trying to make it bigger and better. And do you know what they're bothered about? Teabags!"

Dan laughs while texting on his mobile.

"I mean there's only four months left until the big day and it's a major event to organise. I feel like sending them all an email about our responsibilities as a committee. "

"That presumes some of 'em 'ave a computer, let alone know how to receive an email, love," Dan quickly kisses Vicky on the cheek and heads out of the door.

"True. I've invited some of the, you know, younger ones around for birthday drinks next week though...." Vicky trails off but Dan has gone. By the time Vicky takes off her coat and shoes and closes the door, she can see Dan through her lounge window. Already he is in the pub over the road, ordering his drink at the bar. She goes into the kitchen and opens the fridge. Eight cans of larger, a pre-packed lasagne and half a pint of milk hold little appeal so Vicky flicks the switch of the chrome coloured kettle and makes a dark, black coffee. She opens her laptop and begins to plan her birthday celebrations. A click of a button orders a karaoke machine. Vicky leans back, smiling and hugging her mug of coffee. She surveys the kitchen and despite the disappointments of the evening, Vicky has a look of pride. Clearly imagining the scene of the future party, her gaze wanders from a silver American fridge freezer to a 1950's style juke box. She walks toward the second gadget but catches a glimpse of herself in the reflective door of an integrated microwave. She pauses to take a closer inspection. Vicky narrows her eyes and looks horrified. She grabs a tissue and wipes a puzzling red mark from the end of her nose.

NELL

"I just think that second time around, I'll be so much more relaxed. Not worry so much, you know?"

"Well I'm definitely different this time. And this one's so easy, compared to Callum. Remember how he wouldn't feed, or sleep?"

"I do. You were even more exhausted than the rest of us."

Nell watches the other two women, deep in their conversation and oblivious to her silence. At intervals, she inhales sharply, as if to make a contribution but each time, she fails. Finally, she seems to give up and glances down to the drowsy infant in Rachel's arms. It lies motionless, like draft-excluder along its mother's waistline. Rachel's jumper is raised slightly higher than the baby's head revealing the upper half of a swollen white breast. The child's mouth adheres to it and a wiggling ear is the only sign that she is providing vital nourishment.

Nell's gaze moves to Laura as she wrestles to get comfortable on the sagging red sofa. Every time she leans back, the weight of her enormous stomach is too much and she sits forward again. Nell passes her a cushion and a smile, a smile that remembers how she feels and longs to endure it again.

Three small children play in the corner. An olive-skinned girl prepares a dinner of plastic peas and bananas for her red-headed guest at the miniature, wooden kitchen while a sweaty-looking little boy pushes a dolly in a pram, at speed, towards the television in the corner.

"Callum," sings Rachel, "please don't break Nell's telly-box. She'd be ever so sad."

Nell's mouth smiles at the toddler but her eyes tell him that if he breaks her 32" LED television - which is the only thing she has ever won from the multitude of magazine competitions she enters - she'll take the gingerbread biscuit he's currently smearing all over his face and stamp on it. Hard. "More coffee, anyone?" she manages.

"That'd be great thanks."

"I'd love a water."

Nell escapes the mayhem and heads for the sanctuary of the kitchen. All of a sudden she stops. Her eyes widen as something has clearly taken her breath away. A slow blink, as she turns on her heels, reveals that she is well aware of what has just occurred.

When she reaches the bathroom upstairs, silent tears roll down Nell's cheeks. 'Products of Conception', I heard them tell her to watch out for at the hospital yesterday. 'Products of Conception'. It sounds like the symptom of a flu virus or a chest infection. Something to get rid of. And yet, watching Nell, sitting helpless on her bathroom floor, it is so much more. It is the final sign that her baby has gone. The bloody mass of fibre, lying on a tissue in the palm of Nell's hand, is not identifiably human but it's the closest she will get to what she'd hoped for. She sits for a moment, her gaze frozen on her body's expulsion. In a moment of what must be curiosity or simply a need to know, Nell reaches into the bathroom cabinet for a cotton bud and prods the crimson sack. Ironically, it is impenetrable and strong, protecting the failed inner cells.

"You okay in there?" shouts Laura.

"Yeah," Nell tells them, "Just clearing up a bit. My Rosie's been playing with the toilet roll again".

Abandoning the amateur science experiment, Nell grabs a flimsy nappy bag and places the contents of her hand inside. Securely tied, she pops the bag on the top of the cabinet, and looks in the mirror. Failure, emptiness and rivulets of black mascara stare back. She washes her face, puts her shoulders back and heads back down to the kitchen.

As I struggle to comprehend Nell's masquerade, she busies about, refilling the coffee machine and making a fresh jug of orange squash. The drinks are all placed neatly on a tray and Nell returns to her guests.

"We're doing the whole nappy debate," explains Laura, "I think I'll give the real ones a try this time. You used them with Rosie, didn't you?"

"Er, yes. I did," Nell's eyes widen with concentration as she struggles to descend back into their world.

"I just don't think I could deal with the mess and the extra washing. I mean there's enough of that already. We had to buy a new washing machine last week. The other was only two months out of warranty but I can't complain because we use it so much. I mean, I know real nappies are better for the planet and everything but it's just not for me," Rachel concludes as she removes the sleepy child from her nipple. She pops it on her shoulder with one hand and readjusts her bra strap with the other, like she's been carrying out this rather skilful juggling act all of her life. Remarkably, the child's slumber is undisturbed.

"But you've got to think of all of those, those, big ... holes in the earth," returns Laura.

"Landfills," Rachel assists.

"Sorry, Mummy-brain!" Laura excuses.

"And there's a company who come and collect the real nappies for .." Nell begins to explain but her voice trails off. She looks like she can bear the minutiae no longer. With all my might, I will her to share her experience with her friends, to explain what has happened, to let them understand her pain. And yet she sits silently, allowing them to unwittingly scratch at her wound with every mention of babies and motherhood.

"You okay Nell?" Rachel finally asks.

"Yes, thanks, just tired. We were up late doing the accounts for the restaurant."

"My mother-in-law went last week for the Thursday Night Special. Loved it. Swears it's the best Italian food in Bedston. She said Riccardo was doing the cooking."

"Yes, he lost another chef last week so he's having to manage himself until he can find a new one. Which means he's in the kitchen every hour God sends, leaving me with the accounts and ordering and stuff. But I like to feel like I'm doing my bit," Nell explains. "Talking of which, I've got to go and meet with one of the suppliers in a little while," Nell looks delighted with her brave and unsubtle hint.

As soon Nell's 'friends' have left, she prepares some lunch for Rosie. She uses a scone cutter to make a circular shape with some wholemeal bread before grating cheese to go inside. Purple grapes surround the sandwich she places at the table for her little girl. A squeal of "Flower sandwiches!" makes Nell smile and she sits down beside her daughter. Rosie tucks into the plateful but Nell clearly has no interest in food and gazes up to the kitchen ceiling.

"Mummy must do some decorating in here," Nell informs Rosie who looks puzzled. "Painting, Rosie," she qualifies.

"Painting!" Rosie squeaks and hops down from her chair towards a cupboard. The child opens the door and out pours a plethora of pencils, paint pots and coloured paper. In fright, she rushes back to the table to continue with her lunch, ignoring the fountain still flowing onto the floor.

"No, not that kind of painting, sweetheart," Nell smiles as she tidies up the mess, "Painting on the walls," she can see the mechanics of the child's mind whirring, "but you must never paint on the walls. Just Mummy."

Rosie looks even more confused and rubs her eyes. "Never mind, Rosie-Roo, let's get you up for a nap."

Nell picks up the tired child and heads up the stairs. Rosie's hand drifts along the painted wood chip as they ascend. "Bumpy wall," she observes.

"More decorating to do," sighs Nell.

She places the child in her small pink bed and pulls down the black-out blind at the window.

"Do the song, Mummy," the sleepy creature demands.

"It's a prayer, Rosie, to keep us safe. Are you ready?" Nell's soothing voice, chants words which are clearly familiar to the infant,

"Now I lay me down to sleep,

I pray the Lord my soul to keep.

If I should die before I wake,

I pray the Lord my soul to take."

Nell winds up a small, porcelain ballerina on Rosie's shelf and it plays a soothing lullaby. Rosie gets a dummy from under her pillow, her eyes already closing. Nell heads for the door but stops to look back at her beautiful child. Peaceful in the security of her routine, she is almost asleep already. Nell is drawn back and kisses her head. Temptation is too great and she climbs on to the bed with her daughter. Nestled in the space Rosie has left, Nell lies, holding her most treasured possession. She does not sleep but lies still, knowing she must take comfort from what she still has. Her tears return and this time they are allowed to flow.

Over an hour and a half later, Rosie begins to stir. Like a bird breaking out of its eggshell, she stretches and struggles with the flowery duvet. "Morning!" she greets her mother and Nell instinctively looks at her watch.

"Let's go and see Daddy now, Rosie."

Downstairs, Nell refills her handbag with spare clothes, a beaker of water and two boxes of raisins, while Rosie sits on the stairs trying, with all her might, to put her well-worn shoes on the wrong feet.

"I think they might be more comfortable the other way around, Rosie," Nell advises, obviously keen not to dampen the child's enthusiasm for independence.

"Okay Mummy," she complies, "I just can't do the scarecrow on this one!"

"Scare? Velcro, sweetie, it's velcro!" Nell makes the necessary adjustments and they leave the house.

The bus stop is just outside of their terraced house and the number 57 to Bedston arrives quickly. Three renditions of

"Wheels on the Bus" later, the pair get off near the restaurant. They go past some industrial sized bins, through a narrow alleyway and arrive at a door at the rear where Riccardo is leaning against the wall, smoking. Nell shouts, "Ric!" and shoots her husband a disapproving look which makes him immediately stamp on the cigarette and pick up his daughter. He swings her around in an upward spiral and then holds her up to the sky, kissing her stomach and making her giggle.

"How are you two?" asks Ric. His daughter's continuing yelps of delight qualify as her response and then he turns to his wife. Nell shakes her head. Her eyes well. "Bambino, go see if Jeanette has bread sticks." Rosie runs inside towards a young waitress who bends down to greet the toddler. Ric holds Nell and the silence speaks the words which cannot explain what has happened.

"So it has definitely gone?"

"Don't say it like that," Nell snaps and pulls away from the embrace.

"Sorry, I ... I just mean there's no chance you're still pregnant now at all. Are you certain it's aborted?" Two strong hands regain contact with Nell's shoulders.

"Aborted? You make it sound like this was something you wanted to happen." Nell retreats a step, "The word is 'miscarriage' Ric." She calms down and, for a moment, realises her anger is not with her husband or his linguistic terminology. "The hospital wants to do one last HCG test but yes, I'm certain."

Silence returns.

"Say something then," Nell demands.

Ric shrugs, "I don't know what to say. I can't say right thing. I keep saying wrong thing."

I look down at two people in pain, a pain which should bind them together in their grief. Instead, each word spoken irritates and agitates, making the pain increasingly uncomfortable.

"Maybe it all for the best, Nelly. Maybe God says it is not our time, especially the way things are with this place at the moment. We try again soon," he gives his wife a wink and a smile.

Nell is wide eyed. This final blow obviously hurts more than the others and she clearly cannot envisage how her pain could possibly be a blessing.

"Rosie! We need to go," Nell yells as she goes inside to retrieve their daughter from the young waitress, "Thanks, Jeanette."

Ric finally gives up his efforts, lights another cigarette and watches his family walk back to the bus stop.

SHANNON

" 'ow many times do I 'ave to tell you people? It's *Shannon*, not *Sharon*," an exasperated voice yells across the noisy room.

"That's not what it says on this register," responds a young man wearing a cheap grey suit, which is at least one size too big for him. He shuffles and neatens a pile of A4 paper, in an attempt to convey control over the situation but he's going to have to do better than that, I fear. Most of the names on his 'register' haven't even noticed that he is perched on the edge of a large wooden desk in front of them.

"But I told you yesterday, it's *Shannon*," she maintains his gaze and slowly eases herself forwards, a lioness weighing up her prey, "Or 'ave you forgotten that you took our Geography lesson too, you moron?" Silence descends on the previously raucous classroom and the spotlight shines on this, more interesting, conversation.

"Don't you take that tone with me, young lady," comes the defiant, yet calm, reply. He will not be eaten by this predator.

"Fuckin' supply teachers!" she pounces but looks down to the floor with a knowledge that she will now have to suffer the consequences of her attack.

"That's quite enough. Who's your Head of Year?"

"It's alright. I'm doin' one anyway. Gotta red card, 'aven' I?" Shannon snarls and flashes her escape ticket at the grateful young teacher.

The door slams on the erupting laughter of Shannon's classmates and she takes a familiar walk down the long quiet corridor. Shannon pauses and knocks on a door signed 'Mr Howden: Head of Year 11'. "Come in!" she is ordered.

Inside is different to the classroom and the corridor. The office is tidy yet it feels homely; a money plant and a photograph of two moon-faced children sit on the desk. Like a coat of arms, on the wall behind the desk, is a golden frame surrounding a map which plots every city, town and village in Wales. A window is open and a white net curtain beckons in clean air from the outside world.

"Ah, Miss Child. What can I do for you today?" Mr Howden is optimistic yet realistic enough to know that it won't be a quick visit. He politely pulls out a padded red chair for Shannon to sit down.

With an air of familiarity she slumps in the chair and looks to the carpeted floor, "I've walked out of History, 'aven' I?"

"What has happened this time? Isn't there a supply teacher taking your class today?"

"Mmm"

"Words, please Shannon, words. I cannot help unless you speak words," Mr Howden is interrupted by the shrill ringing of a telephone, which he answers, then nods and "Mmm"s rather a lot himself. "Yes, I've got her here. Yes, I see," he concludes.

"I think I've got the gist," he relays as he slowly puts the handset down. "So, I'm pleased to see that you're using the red card to get out of confrontational situations." The word "but" silently reverberates around the office as it predicts the teacher's next sentence. "But, your use of language wasn't entirely appropriate, was it Shannon?"

"What?"

"I think you know what I mean. We discussed the use of the 'F' word in our last session, didn't we?"

"Oh, that," Shannon recollects. I'm not sure she even knows she's saying it sometimes. It truly carries no more weight than any other word in her vocabulary. "But I didn't tell him to

"Fuck off", I jus' said "Fuckin' supply teachers"." I think I see the difference, subtle as it is.

"Well, that is an improvement but what on Earth required that outburst?" Mr Howden ventures.

Shannon wraps a dirty fingernail around a strand of improbably blonde hair to aid her memory, "He called me Sharon."

"But that *is* your name," Mr Howden winces and seems rather taken aback at his own bravery.

"No-one calls me that though, not even you."

"No. I've learned better," he sighs and wanders to the back of the office. With one hand on his leather belt which lies snugly below his protruding stomach and the other on his furrowed forehead, Mr Howden is clearly planning his next move very carefully. Strategy in place, he turns back to Shannon. "I have to say that I'm really disappointed, Shannon. You know, I thought we were making progress. There have been hardly any 'incidents' this last term and a few of your teachers have even commented that you're just about on your target grades."

"What? E grades and D grades? A lotta bloody good that'll do me."

"But as we've said before, it's all about progression. If you're on target now, and work really hard next half term, who knows what the actual exams will bring? Maybe a few C grades? It's not beyond the realms of possibility if you put the work in. We've got to remain focused and aim high," Mr Howden looks at his watch and then turns back to Shannon. "It's 2.30 now. I don't want to disrupt that supply teacher again by putting you back in the lesson and the Inclusion Unit is full. So I'm going to ring home and see if your dad will pick you up early like we've done before."

"Step-dad," Shannon corrects.

"Yes, yes," Mr Howden makes another phone call and then continues to plough through the mountain of paperwork he was working on before this interval. An invisible Shannon remains slouched in her chair and is now able to chew the gum she has been concealing during the entire previous conversation. She uses the fore finger on her right hand to pick out the dirt from underneath each fingernail on her left hand. She repeats the process with her other hand, wiping the debris on the arm of the red chair. Fully manicured, her forefinger returns to its maypole dancing around her ratty hair.

Almost fifteen minutes later a flustered looking man, who seems hardly old enough to be responsible for Shannon, enters the room. He rubs an emulsion painted hand on his already filthy jeans before offering it to Mr Howden. The teacher hesitates but accepts the gentlemanly greeting and begins to recount Shannon's afternoon. "So in everyone's interests, I think it better if she just goes home a little early and comes back to a fresh start tomorrow," he concludes.

"Yeah, mate, I mean, Sir, Mr Howden. Really sorry, like. She won't be causin' you no more bother, I swear," promises Shannon's step-father and the two exit the room.

The car journey home is awkwardly silent. Shannon puts the radio on. Her step-father switches it off. "What'd you do that for?" Shannon asks.

"Shut it," is the only explanation.

On arrival at their house, Shannon dashes out of the car, pushes open the front door and is about to run straight upstairs when a voice bellows, "Oi!"

She stops in her tracks and re-routes to the lounge. There her mother sits, curled up on a chair, watching a toddler, who is watching *In the Night Garden*. "What 'appened this time then?"

"Nothin'," she shakes her head.

"Can't be bloody nothin' if they sent you 'ome again, can it?" Shannon's mother raises her voice but no other part of her body.

"I 'ad a bit o' bother with a supply teacher," she confesses, "He was crap anyway we weren't gonna learn nothin' ".

"That it? It's shit that school, Shannon. I'm glad you've only got a few months left. Since you're 'ome, love, would you mind watchin' Jack while I 'ave a bath? My back's killin' me," and with that she departs leaving her two children watching television.

"Have you sorted her, Stacey?" Shannon hears from the hallway.

"Yeah, somethin' an' nothin', Rob," her mother dismisses.

"Somethin' an' nothin'? Is that it? I get called away from a big decoratin' job, embarrassed in front of her Head of Year and she's sittin' watchin' *Upsy fuckin' Daisy?* Not bloody likely," Rob is still exploding as he comes into the lounge.

"If your mother isn't going to say nothin' then I am," Rob stands, towering over the teenager, "I'm sick of it Shannon. You think this family revolves around you. You can't behave yourself at school. You can't behave yourself at home."

"Behaving? That's rich coming from you," Shannon retorts then adds in a much lower voice, "I've 'eard them talking about you, you know." She stands up, brushes past him and runs up the stairs. Rob is lost for words and Jack continues to sing with *Iggle Piggle,* entirely unaware that he is now under the watch of his third guardian in as many minutes.

Having tested the strength of every floor board across the landing, Shannon slams her door with a force that shakes the whole house. She flops on to her bed and reaches under to grab a laptop. It has not been switched off since this morning and one press of a button reignites a colourful screen, which is host to a multitude of miniature photographs and row upon row of black words. Shannon begins to type. The white box she is filling reads, "SHANNON CHILD: dad jus had bennie bout naff all had enuf whos up 4 gettin wasted tonite?"

The bait is set and it is not long before a select few of Shannon's hundreds of electronic 'friends' - who by now will be on the school bus home reacquainting themselves with their stowaway mobile phones - enquire about her emotional wellbeing. Finally, she satisfies her appetite for moaning, for berating authority and above all, for being the object of other people's care and concern.

SARAH

"So why exactly is it that when I press the calorie counter and it says I've burnt off the equivalent of say, an apple, the last thing I fancy eating is a piece of fruit?"

"So have the chocolate, Sarah. I don't care; I love you just the way you are," comes the reply she would have predicted but doesn't want to hear.

Nonetheless, Sarah's attempt at a smile is an effort to appreciate Tim's compliment, albeit clichéd. But from what I've seen, it's not helping much. She lies, stretched along the entire length of the brown, leather sofa and rolls, with a groan, to reach the remote control on the floor. Clutching it tightly, a 'V' shape slowly descends on Sarah's brow as her eyes focus on the television screen. *The One Show* provides temporary absorption from the real worries of the day. An article on which seeds to sow in your greenhouse at this time of year is almost interesting.

"Do you want the usual Sarah?" Tim checks as he grabs his wallet from its usual spot on the coffee table.

"U-huh," she dismisses before pausing the TV and watching Tim saunter down the driveway. When he is absolutely out of sight, Sarah dashes up the stairs, quicker than I've seen her move all day, goes into the bedroom and grabs a white paper bag, which she unwraps during the journey across the landing. The bathroom door is firmly shut and locked as Sarah sits on the closed toilet seat.

Shaking fingers fumble with a cellophane cover, then a cardboard box. Sarah unfolds an instruction sheet and makes a photocopy in her head. Instant recognition and familiarity mean that there's no need to read properly but she scans it just the same. In this private game of pass-the-parcel, a foil envelope gives way to the Holy Grail. The truth teller. The life changer.

Sarah lifts the toilet lid and squats over the bowl. Her face grimaces as her Gluteus Maximus aches from its earlier exertion. As the torrents descend, Sarah's hand follows, waving her magic wand at the yellow liquid. She shifts her weight to the left. She shifts her weight to the right. When she has co-ordinated the little white stick with the flow, or what's left of it, there is finally a moment of still.

"Shit!" she proclaims as the stick is brought out of the toilet bowl. Sarah's right hand is dripping and yet she waves it around in an indecisive attempt to put the stick down somewhere. Finally, she settles for the top of the cistern and waddles to the basin, baggy trousers still enveloping her ankles. She quickly washes and dries her hands before rectifying her rather undignified lower half. Unable to wait any longer, she darts straight back to the cistern to see what is happening. Colours change on the screen and a line appears. Sarah checks her watch. It's less than a minute since she first looked but for her it obviously seems like an eternity. Then she looks back at the stick. Nothing changes. The watch. Two minutes. The stick. Nothing. The watch. Three minutes. The stick. Still nothing. She consults the instruction sheet again and confirms that she needs the crucial second line to appear. Another minute. Just in case. Nothing.

Sarah slowly wraps up the whole ordeal in the original white paper bag and breathes right to the bottom of her lungs. She wipes the top of the cistern with a piece of toilet paper and slowly heads back downstairs.

In the kitchen, Sarah opens the fridge door wide and peers inside. She takes out a bottle of Chardonnay, the bottle she clearly had hoped to be able to decline tonight. Instead she pours a large glass and gulps half, quenching her emotional thirst. After refilling, she puts the rest of the bottle back in the fridge and scans the rest of its contents. A slice of last night's pizza sits, calling to her. She demolishes it and quickly hides the evidence in the bin.

"Honey, I'm home!" rings Tim's less than original catchphrase. He kisses the top of Sarah's head and opens a cupboard to get two plates. A pile of rice that would feed a family in some countries for a week, is heaped onto each, before a vermilion volcanic eruption gushes from a silvery tray. In silence, they take their load into the lounge, focusing on the culinary challenge ahead.

When every last scrap of food on their plates is demolished, the pair put the crockery on a coffee table in front of them and sink back into the sofa. "I'm so full," Tim shares.

"I did a pregnancy test today," Sarah blurts out.

"Oh, really? I didn't realise it was that time of the month again already. I'm sorry I didn't ask before now. I just, you know, assume you'll keep me posted and .." Tim's hands wave around, searching desperately to find an excuse for his ignorance.

"Stop twittering, Tim. I've told you before I don't have a 'time of the month'; I'm really irregular. I just felt different, you know. Anyway, it was negative. We're not pregnant. Again. Must've all been in my head," she awaits his response.

"Are you sure? Could the test be wrong?" Tim is hopeful.

"Nah, doubt it. I just don't think I'm ovulating. It's classic of my polycystic ovary syndrome. I see it at work all the time," she dismisses.

"But you've been doing the exercise and losing weight and we've been eating more healthily," he laughs and nods at their empty plates, "Well mostly!"

"It's not funny, Tim. I've been rubbish. The doctor said the best way of increasing our fertility and our chances of having a baby is to lose weight and what do I do? Carry on having Chinese takeaway every Friday night," a disgusted finger points to the plates, "It's all my own fault. I don't deserve a child."

"Oh, don't say that, babe. Self loathing won't get you anywhere. You're doing your best. Neither of us have ever been a friend of salad!" Tim taps his rotund abdomen.

"Well you certainly don't help, Tim. Anybody else would stop me from eating such crap and support me a bit more," Sarah snaps.

Tim pauses his verbal attempts to comfort his wife and reaches out an arm around her shoulder, "Getting yourself all stressed out isn't going to help."

Sarah is almost propelled from the sofa and stands looking down at Tim, "Stop being so bloody nice, would you? I'm off to bed. I'm on earlies in the morning."

A stunned Tim puts his feet in the hollow Sarah has made in the sofa and reaches for the remote control to change the channel on the television.

Half a can of lager later, it seems to occur to Tim that this is not where he ought to be and he heads slowly up the stairs. The bedroom light is off so he fumbles around, getting undressed in the dark. "Brrr.. it's freezing tonight," he tests to see if Sarah is still awake. There is no response. Fully undressed, he climbs under the duvet and shifts towards the body mass lying in the middle of the bed. Realising Sarah is facing the opposite direction, he curls his body around his wife's back and softly kisses her neck. There is still no response. With a futile sigh, Tim also turns over. The two are still. I can feel nothing but sadness from my vantage point, as I see two pairs of staring eyes looking into the abyss of the dark, cold night.

A few short hours later, Sarah gets on to the Tube and sits down next to a man in a black suit. He opens his newspaper beyond the imaginary line which separates their personal space. So Sarah is forced to edge further towards an elderly woman on the other side. I cannot understand how she can be so close as to smell the stale breath of these strangers and yet distance herself from the one she loves. After only a few pages of a novel, she arrives at her stop and walks a short distance to an imposing building with a sign reading *St Mary's Hospital*. As if by magic, two glass doors part to welcome her entrance into the warmth inside. Sarah presses the button to call for the lift but just as it arrives, she turns and walks away, ascending the three flights of stairs to her final destination.

Ward 11 is alive. Even at this early hour of the morning, there is no quiet: telephones ring, babies cry and women chatter, celebrating of the miracle they have all now shared. Here, the world has stopped for a moment. It has abandoned all other aspects of life and these females are united in what they now see as the sole purpose for their existence. Sarah pauses as a new mother heads unsteadily for the bathroom, holding a wall rail as she goes. "Let one of us know if you need a hand with anything," she offers. A nod and a smile are returned. Across the ward a middle aged lady cautiously changes the nappy of a small infant, as her exhausted, teenage daughter sleeps in the bed. A tiny baby in a transparent plastic box is wheeled in front of Sarah, "Morning meeting in five. I'm just getting this one back down to Special Care," the driver informs her.

"Thanks Nana," replies Sarah as she looks at the white board and the computer to assess her day ahead.

Nana returns and calls her staff around the desk. As she updates them on the tribulations of the previous evening, they listen attentively, memorising the names and medical conditions that have changed since their last shift. "God bless you all!" Nana commands and they all return to work.

"Sounds like it's been fun in here last night," says the midwife standing next to Sarah, "Kids eh? Who'd have 'em?"

ME

I watch. I wait. I hear. I listen. I try to make sense.

I am a silent audience, watching four plays unfold. I am in awe of these actors in their moments of glory, when the spotlight shines and they deliver an award-winning performance. But I am also there in the lines they forget, when I yearn to whisper the words they need to carry on. When they triumph, I want to applaud and yet sometimes I am so repulsed that I can barely look. If only I could pull down the curtain and pause for an interval, to make them see, to make them re-audition. But Life's not like that. There is no rehearsal; no second chance. For each one of them, this is it. The Big Show. The One Shot. And I, more than anyone, should know about that.

Working out why I am observing these seemingly ordinary lives has been my sole quest recently. At first, I couldn't quite remember if I knew these people or if they knew me. When I realised they were complete strangers, I wondered if I was some sort of detective, ensuring they abide by the laws of the land. Then I thought maybe I was a spy, who had to feed back my findings to some sort of authority. My whole existence and purpose seemed hazy and unclear, with these questions swimming around and around. When I realised that no-one could even see me, no matter how close I got and that no-one asked me what I had seen, it came to me, that I was simply watching. Through my observations, I have guessed where these lives are heading and with that, I have predicted the possibilities of my own future. Whether I will be the one to make the choice or it will be made for me, I am aware that there are major decisions ahead.

And so I watch them, for no-one else, only for me, and perhaps, if they are fortunate enough, in time to come, they will reap the rewards of my silent endeavours.

In truth, I was never really sure my state was possible until now. I mean, I'd thought about it. I'd even talked about it with others but I'd never truly believed. I am neither animal nor mineral. I am not dead or alive. I am something extraordinary. In the literal sense of the word, I am 'extra', additional, further to anything that I previously would have regarded as 'ordinary', common or normal. Indeed, I am suspended between one life and the next. My past has ended but my future has not yet begun. I am hovering, awaiting a conclusion about where I should land.

In all my wildest dreams, I could not have imagined what this would be like. I don't float on a cloud, or run with the whisper of the breeze. No, I'm just here. Without shape or weight, age or gender, I am liberated, free from all of society's labels and shackles. And yet I know I have purpose. There are no rules or instructions that I am aware of but I am catapulted, magnetically between my subjects, with an inherent knowledge that one of them will be chosen. I have an opportunity to try again, in the rarest of circumstances, to return in human form and be alive once more.

When I first came here, into this No Man's Land of life, I had no memory of my arrival or the journey which surely must have preceded. But gradually I have recalled parts of my untimely deaths and scenes play over in my head which can only come from lives which have gone before. Why they remain with me, I do not know. Maybe they are simply fading. After all, light is not quickly extinguished at the close of day. Rather the sun sets and casts a beautiful glow with the promise that tomorrow it will return. Or maybe I must take instruction from my memories: how to be born, how to live, how to die. Perhaps there are lessons I can learn and like my subjects, maybe I could improve my performance in life's next play.

The lives I observe are very different to anything that I remember in my dreamy recollections. There is nothing familiar in the clothes they wear or the houses they live in. They communicate in a language that would have felt alien to my tongue. And yet I understand their speech. As I hear each word, it becomes untangled from sound and simply retains a meaning, a meaning that can be shared and understood by any human on Earth. With this universal skill, I could be drawn to any subjects on the planet. But the chosen ones are not spread so far. I am the foreigner; they share a language and a heritage. They are different but have so much in common. I do not know the chosen one but I know the culture in which my future lies. Is it this which is my purpose? Am I a pupil of their lives or can they learn from mine?

I have an urge to live their lives, just for a day. I need to feel what they feel, see what they see. Maybe then I will know my destiny. A sudden force is pulling me into a body. My wandering mind is now locked up within a physical shell once more. It is an unfamiliar but comforting sensation, like looking at photographs of an old, childhood home. New eyes and ears make sense of this strange world and new thoughts are imposed on my own. I have become someone else. I am her. Then, like switching channels on television, I am another. My movement between my subjects is fluid but swift, absorbing snapshots of their lives.

VICKY

So that's the karaoke machine here then, thank you very much Mr Delivery Man. I can't wait to try it. Mum's always said I should have been a singer. A pop career is too late for me now though, I guess. Although you never know, these days, with so many reality TV shows. Maybe I should give it some serious thought and apply to one or two next year. That would make those self important arseholes at work notice me, wouldn't it?

Dan's got the drinks covered. He said he's picking them up from the supermarket tonight, didn't he? I hope he gets enough of everything. There's nothing more embarrassing than someone asking for a drink you haven't got. Maybe I'll give him a quick call in a little while to check what he's getting. I must remember to pop over to the pub to collect those extra glasses they said we could borrow.

That just leaves the house. After my superwoman whizz around with the vacuum cleaner, I think it looks tidy enough. Well, the bathroom's clean anyway. I wouldn't want anyone from the village seeing anything less than an immaculate toilet. I'm not so bothered what my old friends think - they've been to the house loads of times - but could you imagine the likes of Barbara and

Frances swapping notes about my dirty loo seat in the playground on Monday morning? I'd be horrified.

I wonder who will actually come. Barbara and Frances seemed pretty keen at the meeting. Bet they never do anything exciting on a Friday night. Maggie said she's coming and if she forgets, I'll see her in the pub from our lounge window and give her a text or send Dan across for her. The gym girls are a definite. I think they've got a birthday surprise for me because they stopped talking really quickly when I came into the changing room yesterday. Less exciting, I'm sure I heard Dan say he'd felt obliged to invite his sister and her latest boyfriend, which will mean his parents will turn up too. I wish my Mum was near enough to come. Ah, well, at least Eliza will be here. If all else fails, and no-one's talking to me, at least I can count on her.

The big decision is what to wear. I've got that black cat-suit from Christmas. I don't think anyone who's coming has seen me in that. I'm sure I only wore it for the Christmas Do. And the work lot are certainly not invited. Imagine the Freddock lot meeting them. They'd have absolutely nothing nice to say about me. Yes, the cat-suit it is. My boobs look fabulous in that and it goes with those silver heels I got last week. Hair up and red lippy, I think.

All that remains is to plan how I'm going to ask Dan. When I think about it, I get that dizzy feeling in the pit of my stomach. The one that rises up your digestive tract and means that your mouth won't speak without the words sounding wobbly. Maybe that's how they'll come out when I ask him. Wobbly. No, they can't. That would sound awful. I must appear mega confident. How will I put it? Do girls ask in the same way as men? *Will you do me the great honour..?* No, that sounds stupid. It's not really me. None of this is really me, I suppose. But it's now or never. I mean, I know it's not the February 29th today but it is a leap year and it's also Valentine's Day and my birthday. So it doesn't get much more romantic than that. No-one will forget it, that's for sure. And if I wait for Dan to do the deed, well, I'll be a very old lady. No, it has to be tonight, dizzy stomach or not. Come on Vicky. You can do it.

NELL

Happy Valentine's Day to me. I know it's just a load of commercial rubbish but I can't help feeling a bit deflated about it all. I think it's just because those mums at Toddler Group kept going on about all the romantic places their husbands were taking them tonight and the lovely gifts they'd been given this morning. Oh, well. It's not like Ric is going out and having fun. Valentines' is one of his busiest nights of the year, after all. And financially, we could definitely do with a few more busy nights. I should be used to it by now. It's no different to any other year. It must just be the hormones.

Having said that, the blood test yesterday said that my HCG levels are dropping to negligible now so I'll have to stop using that as an excuse soon. It doesn't stop it hurting though. I can't concentrate on anything; losing the baby is all I can think about. There's that half a second in the morning when I wake up and forget, or should I say don't remember. And then that's it. It's on my mind when I'm making breakfast, when I'm getting dressed, when I'm playing with Rosie. It's got to the point where my head aches.

I can't help wondering where it all went wrong. Was it that extra cup of coffee the day I was really tired? Or the brie ciabatta I ate before I knew I was pregnant? Or even the stress of having a husband who owns a restaurant in a time when people really can't afford to eat out very often? I know they say that it was probably nothing I did but they would say that, wouldn't they? Otherwise why would medical science advise pregnant ladies to avoid certain things? There must be a reason they do that. If only I could put the clock back and do things differently, be more careful. At least then I wouldn't have this awful guilty feeling gnawing away at me twenty-four hours a day.

It just spins around and around in my head. The middle-of-the-night moments are the worst, when I try to imagine what the baby would have looked like. It would have had Rosie and Ric's warm brown skin, I know that. But would it have had their curls or my straight hair? I think I might have had a little boy this time. Maybe I can't carry boys. I know some people are only successful with certain genders.

I must try to think about other things or I'm going to go mad. After all, I am lucky to have Rosie. She makes me smile each day and brings so much sunshine into our lives. At least I know it's possible for me to have a baby. But in many ways, that makes it all the harder. I know what it is to love a child, to give birth to a being that I love more than living itself.

I'm lucky to have Ric too. Although at the minute it feels like he's a stranger. I know he's distracted by the restaurant and money, or lack of it. But surely this is more important than anything else. We've not even really talked about my miscarriage. And when I try he just says all the wrong things. He just goes on about trying again, like buying another lottery ticket when you've not won. But how will another baby ever replace the one we've lost? I actually don't think I could go through all of this again. And if there's any chance it could happen a second time, well, maybe we just count our blessings and be content with one, beautiful daughter.

Is that the time? We must get going. I said we'd meet Rachel in the park to feed the ducks at ten thirty. Somehow, it's not as bad seeing Rachel with her baby. I'm happy for her, really I am. I just struggle when Laura's there with her bump, all glowing and expectant. She's at her mum's house today so it will be much easier.

SHANNON

Could this week get any sicker? First, Howden puts me in Inclusion for three days for swearin' again. Trust Lucy Fartford - or what ever she's called - to be nickin' one o' me crisps at breaktime just as Pervy Peckham walks past. I mean I like Lucy. We've been 'avin' a good crack in English 'cos we're the only girls but you've gotta say somethin' when someone nicks a crisp 'aven' you? An' *she* knew I was only jokin' when I shouted "Fuck off you silly tart!". But *not* Pervy Peckham. No, *he* marches me straight to Howden sayin' I've been abusive to other students. Then Howden thinks *he's* gotta do somethin' serious about it 'cos it was Pervy Peckham who told 'im. I'm sure those two are bummin' each other or somethin'.

But actually, what they don't know is that I'm dead pleased I'm in Inclusion. It's well safe. No-one bothers me to do work or anythin'. I mean, the teachers are meant to send stuff for us to do but they can never be bothered. So I can just sit there an' 'ave a think, sort stuff out, y'know. I went on the computer yesterday but you're not allowed internet access or messagin', just school games so there's no point in that.

An' there's this well tidy Year Ten lad, who looks much older than a Year Ten, called Evan Jones, who had a fight with a boy in Year Nine, so he's in there too. I've caught 'im starin' at me loads. But I shouldn't be lookin' back an' I defo won't today 'cause me an' Rhys are up to our three month anniversary. I can't believe it's been a whole three months since he asked Sian to ask me out when we was all getting wasted at the park. I remember I wasn't sure at first 'cause I'd always thought he was a bit quiet and with 'im 'avin' left school and everythin', I didn't think he'd be interested in a Year Eleven. But when he came over and chatted to me and I got off with 'im, he was dead sweet and walked me 'ome and made sure I had some chewin' gum so I didn't smell of cider when I got in. Not that they'd've given a shit but I thought it was kind anyway.

And now, red roses on Valentine's Day! I feel proper grown up. When I opened the door and the delivery lady was standin' there, I thought she'd got the wrong 'ouse. No-one's ever got flowers 'ere before. Rob would never send mum flowers 'cause he says they're a 'bloody waste of money'. But she checked the address and sure enough, she'd got the right one. I was gobsmacked. I still am. They're amazin'. They must've cost a fortune, especially on Valentine's Day. This seals it. Rhys is definitely 'the One', sending me flowers an' everythin'. Oh, they've got a proper gift card on them. Let's 'ave a look and see what he's put, *To R from S x*. The daft bastard's only gone an' got our initials the wrong way round. Never mind, it's the thought that counts. I'll go text 'im now an' tell 'im I got them.

What to put? "ta 4 roses will giv u ur prez ltr ;)". There. Send. Oops. I 'aven't got 'im a present. An' that does sound a bit funny when I look at it now. Maybe he'll think I mean we'll *do it* later. Maybe we'll 'ave to *do it* 'cos I can't get into town to buy 'im anythin' before I meet 'im when he finishes at the garage at five.

These'll need some water, I suppose. I'm sure Mum's got a vase round 'ere somewhere but I can't find it. That pint glass'll 'ave to do. If I just chop the bottom off the roses and make the stalks a bit smaller, they'll not fall out. They're really tough though. And sharp. Ouch. Got a bloody cut on my finger now. "Mum! I need a plaster."

SARAH

What a busy night that was. If I hear another screaming baby or another moaning mother ... Who am I trying to kid? I'd give my right arm ten times over to be that mother moaning about her screaming baby. Every time I hear them complaining that they're exhausted after being in labour for two days, or that they've had no sleep during their child's first night on Earth, I want to tell them to count their blessings and simply enjoy that special time because not everyone is that lucky. But they wouldn't understand and I don't expect them to. It wouldn't be very professional either so I just smile and make sure that they, and their babies, are okay.

I'm coming to the conclusion that it's just not meant to be, that my procreational days are over. I guess that God put some of us on the Earth to be mothers and some of us to help others be mothers. And I'm definitely in the latter category. I mean, who would be telling a labouring woman which position will make her more comfortable, or teaching a new mum the best position for her baby to latch on, if it wasn't for us lot? At least I get to spend time with babies and to feel part of that wonderful experience. If I had my own kids, I'd be constantly juggling my family life with work and probably doing a bad job of both, if some of my friends are anything to go by. That's if I made it back to work at all. I'm good at what I do and I feel needed. This is my place in the world.

Indeed, the time has come to focus on me and Tim. I know I've been snappy with him the last week or two. I can hear how unreasonable I sound when I speak to him and I sense him biting his tongue for fear of upsetting me more. But I've just felt under so much pressure to be pregnant. When we got married, it just seemed like the next step, to start trying for a family of our own. Gradually, all of our friends who got married around the same time have announced their new arrivals and Tim's parents have made very unsubtle hints about 'the pitter patter of tiny feet'. And it truly has been what we have wanted too. To make a new life with the person you love and watch it grow and fill your home with laughter and play would be literally quite awesome. But maybe there is more to life. We got married to be together, and love one another, so to ruin that all by obsessing about a third person, seems crazy.

We should put all of this heartache behind us and start a new chapter. I mean, we can start spending some of that "Baby Pot" he's been saving from his bonuses. Exotic holidays could become a new hobby of ours. Just because all of our friends are having families doesn't mean that we have to follow suit. We can be happy without children.

Even thinking these thoughts feels like I have eased my burden a little, lightened the load. I'm going to speak to Tim about how I feel and I'm certain that eventually he'll see that I'm right. We'll chat over lunch before his flight. It's not like Tim to be so romantic as to take me to posh restaurants for lunch but I think he feels bad about leaving me on my own on Valentine's night. I don't mind at all really. He's been looking forward to Gaz's Stag Do for ages and the time away will be good for both of us.

I'm planning a warm bath, a good book and a glass or two of red tonight. See, I couldn't do that if I'd been pregnant. Indeed, today is the start of the new me.

ME

My strange experience has left me feeling dreadful. I am disorientated, I lack any clarity of thought and worst of all, I am still uncertain of my future. For such a long time, I watched these women and now I have briefly *been* these women but which one is right for me? I do not know. From what I have seen, I cannot imagine belonging to any of them. How on Earth can I possibly be born to a ferrel teenager who thrives on the attention gained by flouting authority? And the others, although more mature in their years, are little better. One is so externally referenced and influenced by what others think that she could never prioritise the needs of a child before her own. Another is stricken with grief for a lost soul and as a result, is submerged in a world which is not fit for my entrance. The last has so little will power or control that she has given up all hope of becoming a mother. There is simply no harmony in any of these lives and certainly no attraction for this sorry soul. If this is my lot, I need to go back, to delve further into their worlds and to learn more. I must continue to go from one to another and look through their eyes until I know them like I knew my former selves. Only then will I know where this journey ends and which mother will bring me into her sphere.

VICKY

I couldn't be more pleased with how that went. My party was every bit the success I knew it would be. Lying here, I must be the most contented woman in Freddock. How many people can say that they're so happy that they can't sleep? Well, Dan's snoring isn't helping either, bless him. I just keep re-living the evening over in my head. It gets better every time, like a good chic-flick on a girly night in.

If I do say so myself, I looked sensational. Lots of people admired the cat-suit, although I must have put on a couple of pounds since Christmas as it was starting to restrict my breathing by the end of the night. As they say, pride is painful. All that time I spent doing my hair and make-up really paid off and I'm proud that I managed to keep steady on my heels on all night, despite the vodkas. Seems a bit silly, when you think about it, wearing heels to a party in your own house, when you don't intend stepping foot outside. But I wouldn't be seen dead without them.

Anyway, I was pleased that so many people came. Barbara and Frances turned up first. I think they said their husbands were looking after their kids or something. Isn't that what you pay babysitters for? I'm sure it wouldn't keep me in on a Friday night. They're a bit odd but I think I could grow to like them. It was all a bit awkward at first when they insisted on talking about their bloody Parent Teacher Committee - I do wonder how many committees one person can belong to - and which teachers their kids like at school. I thought I might nod off when one of them started listing the spellings their son had this week. They did get a bit more interesting after the large glasses of wine I was pouring though. I've just remembered them telling me about one of the mums from the playground who openly talks about how she's shagging the guy from the Freddock Butcher's shop. And her husband has absolutely no idea. Now that was worth listening to.

I knew Dan's parents would turn up with Emma and Tom. I mean it's not like they're not welcome but we could have had lunch on Sunday with them or something. Parties can't be their sort of thing. I wasn't sure what kind of party they were expecting when she brought that corned beef pie. It totally spoiled the food table and certainly didn't go with my Indian theme. It looked really stupid stuck between the samosas and the tikka bites. And as for Emma and Tom, they're not exactly sociable. I can't believe they sat in the corner, just talking to each other. Mind you, better that than talk to my friends. I don't know what she'd say about me. I swear she doesn't like me. I'm still furious about the way she burst into tears and then went home in the middle of the evening. Talk about an attention seeker.

Poor old Eliza got the brunt of my moaning about Dan's family. She'll always listen though, she's good like that. I'll never forget how she helped me when my dad died. I remember how she'd bring me dinner round to make sure I'd eaten. "I cooked too much so I wondered if you wanted some," she'd say, while opening my curtains and dragging three day old washing out of the machine for me. Lord knows how I'd have survived without her, living in that little flat, in that state, by myself, in my pre-Dan days. I did try to repay the favour when that horrible Baz ran off and left her with the kids. I'm so glad Eliza's picked herself up too now. We're like two different people. I do remember hugging her rather a lot and telling her how much I love her tonight.

Maggie and her husband got here next, I think, in the middle of my Eliza hugging. It was really sweet that they'd skipped dessert at the pub so as not to miss my party. Some of the things she wears are so outrageous. They'd look awful on anyone else, but with Maggie, well, it just works. Take tonight, she had a bright pink satin trouser suit on, the likes of which I have never seen in any shop or magazine. And I'm sure she wears a wig. Never mind, they did bring those two bottles of champagne which came in very handy later on.

I wish I'd looked at my watch to see what time it was when the gym girls eventually arrived and rolled out of their taxi. Anyway, at least they came and I can always count on them to liven things up a bit. Luckily they were quite dressed up too and aren't shy of a drink. So much so that they had to order another taxi to take Mel home early. She seemed alright to me but someone was saying she'd fallen asleep in the loo. Cass did say that they'd intended to stay at least a couple more hours but after all, it would cost less if they all just left together and shared another taxi home. I'm glad I managed to get the karaoke machine switched on before they left. We were fabulous at *Raining Men*, the five of us. No surprise pressie from them, though. Maybe they'll save it for Monday when we meet up for coffee after our spin class.

They definitely left before 11 o'clock because that's when the lads Dan drinks with in the pub came over. They'd clearly been in there since finishing work and said they'd been up for getting a taxi into town to go clubbing, until they'd seen our light on and heard the music. So that was a real compliment that they chose to come over to ours. One of them, I think he's called Mark, was desperate to do a bit of karaoke so I did a duet with him before the others dragged him off into the lounge.

I must've felt a bit more confident, or more drunk, than usual, when I did those solos. I only sang the ones I know I'm good at, the ones Dan says I do okay. The one I did with Barbara and Frances was good fun too. They were a bit microphone-shy at first but they soon warmed up and I think they were glad they stayed that little bit longer after all.

When they said they really must get home, I knew that was my moment. Switching the karaoke machine off but leaving the mic on was a great idea. The lads all came back through to the kitchen really quickly when I said I had an important announcement to make. I'm trying to remember exactly how I put it but I thanked everyone for coming and for helping me celebrate my birthday, that's right.

Taking a deep breath and absorbing the moment, I looked around my fabulous kitchen, in my fabulous home, and thought about how lucky I am. I looked at my black granite work tops, and my centre island with my induction hob, which has been simply begging for a party like this since we had it installed last year. I looked at the people who were sitting at my red, high-gloss bar stools and I caught Frances staring at my low floor unit lights. I had friends around me and the atmosphere was perfect.

"Well," I remember stalling, "There's another reason I wanted to gather everyone we hold dear." Their attention was mine now and I loved every second of it. "I know it's not February 29th, but it is a leap year. And it's Valentine's Day and my birthday. So I felt they were good enough reasons to allow me take the plunge and ask, Dan, *Will you marry me?*"

Sure enough, everyone cheered as much as I'd always imagined and then there was that pause, when I think they all realised that Dan hadn't had a chance to respond. Of course he said "Yes", or at least he must have done - that bit's quite hazy - as the whooping continued. Maggie swiftly remembered the champagne she'd brought and got it back out of the fridge.

And here I lie, smiling and remembering. I don't think life gets any better than this. I've got my house, got my man and soon, I'll get the fairytale wedding I've dreamt about from being a little girl. Ooh, that'll be fun to plan. I must call Eliza in the morning to come round for a glass of wine to discuss my ideas.

NELL

Like my week's not been hideous enough, Fate has to throw in another blow. Trying to piece together bits of today feels like putting together a jigsaw from two entirely different boxes. I remember putting Rosie's red jumper on her and getting ready to go to the park. And I know that currently, I'm here in a hospital bed, on a noisy ward of ill people, feeling rather ropey myself. But in between is just a blur of images. What does that clock say? About four o'clock? I haven't had this kind of memory loss since my student days. At least back then, there was a cracking night out to make it all worthwhile.

When I was getting Rosie dressed, I must admit, I did feel a bit grim but to be honest, I've felt rough for weeks. The morning sickness and sheer exhaustion had already set in before I lost the baby. It was when it all stopped one day and I'd not been up for a wee in the night that I knew something was wrong. And sure enough, the bleeding started that night. And then I've felt rubbish ever since. Lack of proper sleep, I've been putting it down to. But actually, now that I think about it, it did feel a bit different this morning, more like I was getting a cold, sort of fuzzy headed, with waves of hot and cold.

We must have got to the park because more snapshots are coming back to me. I was seething when Rachel and I bumped into that awful Donna woman from Rosie's and Callum's Ante-Natal group. I didn't like her or her attitude when we all used to meet up for coffee and certainly didn't feel like making small talk with her today. I swear she is the most emotionally unintelligent woman I have ever met. Having just given birth to her second child, she was coo-ing and comparing notes with Rachel. Of course, I don't begrudge her that, we've all done it. But the way she turned to me and asked, "Are you not having any more Nell?" defied belief really. I mean, what was she expecting me to say? "No, I only ever want to experience the joys of motherhood - which you know I have loved - once in my entire life" or, "Yes, Ric and I are scheduled to attempt conception tomorrow night when my basal temperatures indicate that I'll be ovulating". Or even, the harsher reality of "Actually, my body repelled an eleven week old embryo last week and I'm still feeling rather traumatised." So I smiled and said, "This one keeps me busy for now". I'm too nice sometimes.

The kids must have been feeding the ducks because I remember having a bag of birdseed in my hand and Rosie spilling it on the grass, then laughing as she ran away from the ducks who came to eat it. But from then on it gets sketchy. Rachel asked if I was okay as I looked really hot and sweaty all of a sudden, so I went to sit down on a bench. But that's when my memory stops. Apparently, according to the nurses, I fainted and Rachel called an ambulance to bring me here.

When I came to in the ambulance, I remember the lovely paramedic kept telling me that my friend had taken my daughter to her house and that I wasn't to worry as Rachel would contact my husband to let him know what was going on. I bet Rosie's having a great time with Callum actually. They'll have thought the ambulance debacle was a huge adventure. I know Rachel will give her tea and even put her to bed for me if needs be.

I hate hospitals with a passion. That chemical smell and the constant noise is nauseating and makes me feel ill rather than better. I must try and remember what the doctor just told me. If I can get this right in my own head now, I'll be able to tell Ric properly. He said that they knew from me fainting and my high temperature that I must have an infection and when they went to look at my notes, the clear conclusion was that it must be coming from my uterus. It would appear that sometimes, after a miscarriage, some of the pregnancy tissue is retained and then becomes infected. What was the procedure called that they're going to take me down for later? A 'D and C' or something, which will clear out my womb. When she comes over, I'm going to ask the nurse more about that because I couldn't really take any more in when the doctor was talking. That's as far as I got. I'm so tired.

I'm sure Ric will listen and remember everything for me when he gets here. I'll get the nurse to try ringing him again. I know they said Rachel would be trying too but I'd have thought he'd be here by now. Unless he's had to pop to the suppliers this afternoon; sometimes his signal is dodgy over that way. Ah, well, I'm sure he'll be over as soon as he hears. I'll have to get him to bring me some better clothes in than this. It's so embarrassing lying here in these old jeans and my fleece. It didn't seem so scruffy for the park but a hospital's different. Mind you, not many of my clothes are new or smart these days. There's always something better to spend money on. I might need a nightie bringing in too if they do take me down to surgery.

Here's the nurse now. I'll ask her all my questions ...

SHANNON

Okay. Think, Shannon, think. You need like a plan or somethin'. But what? I can't talk to me friends 'cos they've all logged off and gone to bed, even Sian who's usually on till eleven when her mam tells her to switch off. What was it old Howden told me? If I'm feelin' mega stressed out and got too much goin' on in my 'ead, I could write it down. I got bollocked for laughin' at 'im when he said it but he's alright really, so it's worth a try. I got one 'o them secret diaries from when I was like nine or somethin'. That'll do ..

'Dear diary
Today started out really good cos I got flowers off Rhys for valentines day or I thought I did I was well chuffed and couldn't stop thinking about him all day even when Evan Jones kept staring at me in Inclusion I even decided we probably would do it tonight me and Rhys that is not me and Evan LOL
When I met him at the shops after he finished at the garage he looked totally fit in his overalls but he was more quiet than normal and funny with me he said he never sent flowers to me and wanted to find out who did so he could smash his face in

I said I didn't know and he said I must know cos people don't just send you flowers for no reason he said it must be someone from school and that's what his mates had always said would happen if he went out with a Year 11

I managed to convince him I didn't know who they was from and that I didn't fancy any of the boys in my year cos they're all like total geeks and freaks

We was finally making up if you know what I mean ;) We was probably going to end up going down the park and doing it but my phone went it was Mum she said she needed me home straight away to bath Jack and put him to bed FFS I mean talk about timing but I'll do anything for my little man he's my number one so I kissed Rhys and went home

Before I even got in the front door I could hear them shouting and screaming at each other I went in and they stopped for a bit Rob just looked at the floor and mum said Jack was watching telly so could I take him up for his bath that's when I knew it was too bad to ask what it was about cos they went into the kitchen and shut the door

Anyway I took my little man up stairs and ran his bath I made it really bubbly and put all his favourite bath toys in just how he likes it I got him stripped and we sang twinkle twinkle about 20 times while he had a nice play I got him some clean pjs on cos I don't think mum has changed them for about two weeks the scruff and then he got a story for me to read I still couldn't hear much from down stairs so I got Jack's dummy and tucked him into bed

When I was coming down the stairs Rob shouted at me "And you may as well come and hear this Shannon" so I went into the kitchen

Mum started telling me how Rob has been seeing this slapper from the chippy called Suzie the one with the orange tan apparently it was her who sent Rob the flowers this morning not Rhys sending them to me :(and then later on a card arrived and when mum asked Rob he didn't deny any of it

So the stupid cow was like begging the twonk to stay and finish with the fake bake and I was like Mum, have some self respect and chuck him out

That's when it got really bad and he said it he said that none of this would have happened if it wasn't for me. Me? LMFAO what did I do? Make him go and shag the greasy chippy tart? Make her do something stupid like send cards and flowers to our house? FFS Apparently if it wasn't for me being trouble and getting into bother at school and get this, taking too long in the bathroom in the morning FFS then my mum would be happier and easier to live with and he wouldn't have to go and look elsewhere (too much info BTW)

So he was ranting on and Mum was crying then he said that if she really wanted him to stay then I'd have to go go where I asked him but he said he didn't care and he'd had enough of me and it was me or him

The worst bit of it all was that Mum didn't say a word she just kept crying even when I looked at her and begged her to pick me so I came up to my room

Well that's it if she even has to think about it for a second that's not good enough for me I'm off

I could go to Gran's but she's dead old and would want me in bed by like 8 and her spare room smells a bit funny and I don't think she'd ever give me any money for going out what with being on her pension and all and she lives the other side of town so I'd have to get a bus to see Rhys'

That's it. It worked. Thanks Howden, you old bugger. I've got a plan now. Writin' it down did the trick. I'm going to go and live at Rhys's house. He's got like five brothers an' sisters or somethin' so one more won't be a problem. His twin brother has his girlfriend over to stay all the time, Rhys says. I'll text him in the morning. Best get some sleep now then 'cos I bet those two won't hear Jack in the morning and it'll be muggins 'ere who has to get up for 'is bottle.

SARAH

Look at me. I think I look happier. Unless, that is, these toilet mirrors are like the flattering, slimming ones they have in some of the clothes shops which make my mammoth size twenty two body look like an almost respectable size eighteen, and they put roses in your cheeks, whiten your teeth and widen your smile. Where's my lipstick in this mess of a handbag? I must tidy it up when I get home. There it is. That makes an even better picture. Mirror, mirror on the wall ...

I'm so thrilled Tim reacted the way he did today. Although I'm quite surprised how quickly he came around to the idea of us being content without children. It was almost like a relief to him too. Maybe he never really wanted kids in the first place. Now there's a worrying thought. Did I push him into it, I wonder? No, he always seemed so excited when we talked about it and planned our future. And he was never reluctant on the practical side of trying either. Perhaps he was just keeping me happy. That's Tim all over. Oh, I don't know. I think we do need to talk some more when he gets back from the stag weekend but I'm satisfied he's alright with it all for now and it's a weight off my mind knowing I've told him how I feel.

I bet he's thinking of how to spend the 'Baby Pot' too. I'll have to watch out for deliveries of new golf clubs and that fancy computer he's always going on about. I'd best get a holiday booked soon before it's all spent up. I quite fancy Barbados, this year, splash out on a real bit of luxury. One of the doctors at work says it's amazing. Our grown up world is something to really look forward to, however we spend our money and time. Even just lazy weekends reading the newspapers and pub lunches in the countryside seem attractive when there's no underlying wish that it could be different. I must remember to pray for our new future at church on Sunday.

And that meal was fabulous. I could eat my prawn starter all over again and that chocolate fudge cake was to die for. I'm glad Tim's driving so I can finish that bottle of wine before he drops me back at home. There is something to be said for peaceful child-free restaurants too. We'd probably have ended up in fast food outlets every weekend with children. Fine dining would have become a distant memory.

I can't believe it has taken me so long to realise what my priorities are in life. The world expects every married couple to produce offspring and when they don't, they feel like a failure. We are not failures. We are fully satisfied human beings with a wonderful relationship and successful careers. Why should I care what the world wants when all I want is a quiet life, with my husband, enjoying the fruits of our labour? I had become so wrapped up in my baby tunnel that I couldn't see this truth.

I will keep my promise to lose weight though. And I'm going to be serious about it this time. No more take aways, no more chocolate or crisps and I'm going to go to the gym with a better attitude. Victoria Beckham doesn't look that good without a little hard work and sacrifice. Pretending I was eating well and being half hearted about exercise was just getting me down. This is where my downward spiral stops.

Right. Tim's going to wonder what on Earth I've been doing in here for so long. I'm glad there was no-one else in here. They'd've thought I was bonkers, putting my lippy on three times and admiring at myself in the mirror. Nothing wrong with a little but of daydreaming now and again. Anyway, Tim said he was going to ask for the bill. That'll leave just enough time to finish the wine and then Tim'll drop me back at home on his way to the airport.

ME

Oh how I enjoyed that. Once the disorientation has settled, rejoining the human race is actually quite sublime. In my timeless, weightless, shapeless state I had forgotten what it is to be alive. To be real again and to feel again, floods me with desire to be reborn.

To feel Vicky's clothes against her skin reignited my sensations. The cool, silky material enveloped her body and every fibre seemed to tease her nerve endings as she moved throughout the evening.

My senses, once fully awake, became intoxicated when Sarah devoured her lunch. Sweet followed savoury, rough combined with smooth and sent me to forgotten heights of ecstasy. Never before had I appreciated a full culinary experience, from the first flavours detected by the taste buds on our tongues to the divine feeling of satisfaction at the pit of the stomach.

Now on a mission to experience these basic human functions, I tuned into the smells around me. Although Nell despised it, I absorbed the smell of that hospital with a thirst that could not be quenched. Disinfectant pervades, in its attempt to triumph over the others but a keen nose can detect all sorts of other odours in such a place. Bodily excretions are in abundance there: blood, vomit, sweat, urine, faeces. No-one wants to see them or smell them or even admit that they exist but we all know that without them, we could not function as human beings.

I even found great pleasure in listening to Shannon's parents arguing. Of course, my great sadness lay with the plight of the girl and her brother. However, to hear two people so passionate about their point of view that their voices battle for supremacy and invade the silence of all those around them, well, that's significant. To heighten the emotions of another human being is to let them know that they are not alone, that they are eternally intertwined with others in the race.

As if sensing all of the things that these women were experiencing wasn't enough, I began to feel their emotions. When Vicky was preparing to ask Dan to marry her, she had several failed attempts. Every time she thought about pausing the party to make the announcement, I felt a rush of adrenaline through her veins and felt the way it seemed to stop at her pounding heart. When she finally found the courage to see it through, the anticipation of what would happen next was almost too much to bear. Her lips trembled with every word she uttered and her voice altered as her mouth dried. Here I was, perching on the edge of a life changing moment.

Of course these women haven't all had such excitement in their lives today. When Shannon's mother stood by her husband rather than her daughter, the rejection felt almost physical, as if someone had driven a knife into to the poor girl's heart. She is so confused as she enters the adult world and as such, is unable to voice her fears to anyone.

Nell's pain is equally difficult to experience. The wall with which she surrounds herself is impenetrable by others which makes her grief stifling, as it bounces back, unable to escape beyond her self-made barrier. At times, I felt that this overload was sufficient to knock me right back out of Nell's body.

Sarah has travelled an emotional journey of late and her disappointment and feelings of failure have been uplifted by her sudden optimism and hope for the future. She is strong in her faith and believes that her god will provide guidance. I have felt this strength and it is inspiring. To see the best in our lives and to find joy in despair is to step out of a dark hole and run towards the sunrise.

What I still find fascinating about all of these women, however, are their priorities. They value things that were so much less precious to me in former lives. Whether it be a wardrobe full of clothes, or pointless electronic devices, they seem to define themselves and their happiness by what they have and what they own. Vicky spends her life trying to impress the world around her with what she wears and with the interior of her house. Nell's unhappiness is exacerbated because she cannot afford to do either of these things. Sarah feels her life will be enhanced by spending her money and Shannon most certainly would not be able to function without her laptop or mobile phone. In my uncertain state, one thing I do know, is that no-one really finds their happiness this greedy, gathering of belongings and material wealth. As I struggle to understand them, I recall the last days of someone I used to be, someone whose needs were so much more basic ...

JIYA

The months leading up to my end were, as I remember, pleasant enough. Despite our circumstances, my memories are filled with sunshine and laughter. Earlier that year, Pitaa had finally decided to allow us go to school and my sisters and I could not have been more delighted. Maataa had asked him before but every time he had said there was no virtue in educating us. What would we learn from school that would equip us for the rest of our lives? How to be a good wife and look after the children? No, he would say, they shall stay at home and help here.

But then the lady from the Garden School came to visit. She had been going around lots of houses in Dharmapur, telling families about a new opportunity for their children.

"Pah!" Pitaa exclaimed sarcastically, "If it's as good as the anganwadi, we'll all be eternally grateful."

I remembered the previous year when well-dressed people would come to the feeding points and dole out ladles of gruel to me and my sisters as we stood, holding out our tin pots on the hot, dusty street. At first, it was every day. They fed only the children but I could see the relief in Maataa's eyes when we returned with full bellies and she knew that some of us, at least, would not go to sleep hungry that night. One day, we waited in vain, just to return home with shining but unused pots. They did return after that but no-one could predict when and on the occasions they did, the gruel became less and less. Someone in the town told Pitaa that the workers were selling the food for profit in more affluent areas of Bhopal.

"And don't even speak to me about the ration cards," Pitaa broke my day dream, "The government has no idea what life is like for us."

"No, sir," the lady spoke softly, "This will be different. It's not like the government schools. The government will not be involved. The Garden School is entirely charitable and organised through the goodwill and generous donations of our kind benefactors. Your children will be provided with the kind of skills that will help them in whatever job they choose to do when they are older. We will even liaise with employers to ensure that older children are able to combine school with work."

Pitaa continued to fan his face with a grass leaf and Maataa continued to rock Aasha, my youngest sister, to sleep in the corner.

"Your daughters would each receive all of the books and equipment they would need as well as a uniform to wear," the lady looked at the three of us and her eyes revealed her discomfort at seeing Anya and Prisha in their unashamedly naked state. I, a little older, was wearing a dress Maataa had been given by a neighbour, whose older children had outgrown it.

"And your son would be old enough to join them in a year or so," she gestured down to Aadi, who was lying down, making circular patterns in a patch of dust he had uncovered by pushing one of our floor rugs to one side.

"Ahh," she had Pitaa's attention now. Everything was different when it came to Aadi. Two of Maatta's babies had died before Aadi arrived so there were huge celebrations when this boy child was born and made it beyond his first year.

"They will also be given a hot midday meal at no cost to yourselves."

I saw Maataa's eyes light up and dart across the room to Pitaa. The kind lady left shortly after and we were at school the very next week.

Every morning I would get up and get my sisters dressed in their uniform. When I put on my own, it felt hot and constricting but it felt mine. Never before had we owned clothes which had not previously belonged to someone else. When I put on my blue shirt, I felt taller, more important. We each had a deep green cotton skirt which, when rolled at the top, fitted snuggly around our swollen abdomens. In each side of the skirt was a pocket which had little purpose for children with no belongings but made us feel like someone cared enough to make it for us.

Then my sisters and I would wave goodbye to Maataa and the little ones and run to school, joking and laughing all of the way. It was as if our journey to school led us into a different world where food and survival were no longer all we thought about.

Teachers at school were like gods and in my mind were to be worshipped and adored alongside Brahma, Vishnu and Shiva. Certainly, Brahmam had been incarnated on Earth in the form of Miss Steel. She had come over from America for a year to help with our school. Her Hindu was poor at first but that didn't matter; drawing and painting don't require language and the animals and people she showed us how to draw spoke for themselves. As she became more familiar with Hindu, she would sing the words to English songs to us and try to explain their meaning. In return, we would teach Miss Steel Bollywood songs and, when we got a little more confident, show her the dance routines we'd made up in the streets after school. All morning we looked forward to our rice, a refreshing change from the chapati we'd been having at home. Rice had become so expensive that everything had to be made from the small amount of wheat flour Maataa treasured in a can at home.

When we had finished school for the day, my sisters and I would walk home, chattering about how much we had enjoyed ourselves. It was an unsaid rule that this stopped just before we walked in the house. The corrugated metal walls and roof were a far cry from the plaster and paint of the school building. Nonetheless, we changed our clothes and our expectations when we arrived home. Maataa would be still sitting outside sorting the green leaves into bundles ready for the cigarette man to collect and Aadi would have found a shady spot next to her, escaping the scorching heat. She would hug the three of us until we felt like we would suffocate the baby, who was sleeping, wrapped to Maataa, in a faded, black cloth. I would take the baby, Aadi and the girls to play with our friends in the street which gave Maataa time to finish her work and prepare the chapati for supper. We even had some onion and ground chilli for a while so Pitaa's return form work felt like a feast.

This was our steady, contented routine until my last few weeks. I felt like the luckiest girl in the world. I had loving parents, my sisters and brother, food in my stomach and most of all my school and my Miss Steel. If given a wish, I couldn't have thought of anything to hope for.

And then it changed. One day we came home to find Pitaa sitting next to Maataa. Without questioning his presence, my sisters simply embraced him before hugging Maataa. They quickly went to play but I knew there was a reason he was home at this time of day. Usually it was dusk before he returned.

When the smaller ones had gone to sleep that night, I asked Maataa what was wrong. "Nothing, sweet Jiya," she reassured me, "Go to sleep."

In our house, it was impossible to talk privately; no room divisions meant no secrets so I heard their conversations that evening. Pitaa had been doing odd jobs for a man of higher caste who lived in the next town for well over a year now. They were just labouring jobs: sowing the crops, fixing the sheds, that sort of thing. He wasn't paid highly but alongside Maataa's leaf sorting, there was enough money to buy the wheat flour for the week. Pitaa's employer had been killed in a machinery accident that day which meant no more work.

Maataa sobbed and Pitaa comforted.

"What are we to do?" she cried.

"We will pray to Lakshmi for guidance and have faith that the gods will provide for us, if not in this life then in the next."

And with that, I saw the pair move over to our altar and offer the last piece of our supper to the murti.

The following days were difficult. My sisters and I barely suffered as we still went to school and received our lunchtime gift. The baby was fine as Maataa was still able to feed her milk. But Maataa and Pitaa and poor little Aadi ravished their chapati every evening with a hunger I knew came from eating nothing else all day. Aadi grew weak and his dark skin paled when compared to our own. Even in a few short days his stomach ballooned and he became more lethargic than ever.

Knowing that our family faced more hardship than ever, made it almost impossible to concentrate at school. I spent my time thinking of ways I could help. In my darkest moment, I thought about the families of my friends and which ones left their homes unoccupied in the afternoons. I could easily sneak in and take some of their wheat flour. That idea was short lived when I remembered what Maataa always taught us, *It is better to be poor than to be a thief.* I realised that this idea would create terrible Karma for me and so my plan had to be different.

I did it without really thinking one day. When the teacher who served us lunch handed me my plate of rice, I went to sit in the corner of the room with my back to the adults. I quickly filled my skirt pockets with my lunch and sat for a moment to make sure no-one noticed.

All afternoon I was careful not to lose a grain and by the time I returned home, the starchy substance had formed two flat circles. Maataa said Aadi was lying down inside so I went in to see him. His eyes were shut although I could tell he was not asleep. So I called his name and he mustered the energy to smile at me. I sat him up and fed him the rice balls. That night he ate with less ferocity, which was lucky as our chapattis were increasingly smaller in size.

I continued this offering every afternoon. Aadi got better and started to play outside with the rest of us again. Pitaa said it was a miracle and that Lakshmi was looking down on us. Aadi, of course, started to look for his afternoon treat and began to run down the street to meet me and my rice parcels every day.

As Aadi got healthier, I began to feel weaker. I longed for my chapati all day but it was no longer enough and my stomach began to swell more than ever. When I got dressed in the morning, I noticed that my hair was thinning and my skin was lightening a shade. When at last I had no energy to walk, I had to stop going to school.

My memories are few after that time. Breathing was difficult and I have an image of Maataa sitting by my bedside, mopping my brow, telling me I had picked up a virus. She also told me that it was all going to be okay as Pitaa was going up to Delhi to work on the rickshaws and this would buy all the wheat flour we would need. But I knew it was too late for me.

At least Pitaa's boy was saved, I kept thinking. He might go on to have the opportunities that really, were just a fantasy for us girls. Or maybe he won't. I don't know what became of the rest of my family and whether they improved their lot. But I do know that my death, like my life, was happy, secure in the knowledge that I had tried to become closer to Brahman and that in doing do, my soul may be one step further towards freedom.

VICKY

"So, never mind that, are we going to discuss wedding plans or what?" Eliza asks me.

How can I begin to tell her what has happened? Last she knew, we were drinking champagne, celebrating my brave proposal last night.

"Come on, I didn't come round to talk about your summer fair - no offence - but Dan'll be back from the pub at this rate and I'd much rather have your take on it all. Get this bottle opened before it gets warm."

"I've got something to tell you, first," I pause mid-wine pouring. But which version? The official 'Dan' version or the truth? Who am I kidding? It's Eliza. She'll be able to tell if I'm lying. Besides, it would be good to be straight with someone after the day I've had.

"Ooh, come on then," Eliza clearly hasn't picked up on my serious tone.

Here goes. "I've done something really bad, Eliza," I hadn't realised how upset I would get vocalising my actions.

"Hey, honey," her sympathetic arm around my shoulders is making me feel ten times worse. "Nothing can be that bad. Don't let it ruin your special weekend."

"That's just it. It's already ruined. Dan didn't really want to marry me after all." There. I've done the hard bit.

"What? I passed him as I came in just a few minutes ago and he seemed just as delighted as he was last night." Poor Eliza looks as confused as I feel.

"Well, that's not how it's been all afternoon."

"You'd better start at the beginning," I'm glad Eliza's taken over the wine pouring. I'm shaking like a leaf and would spill it everywhere.

"This morning I got up early and made Dan a fry-up. I thought it would be a special kind of day, you know? I thought we'd have breakfast then go back to bed and spend the rest of the day talking about getting married. How stupid was I?"

"Don't say that."

"Well anyway, he came down and just looked at his breakfast. He said he didn't want it and that's when I knew something was wrong; Dan loves fried food. Even more out of character, he asked if we could talk. I stopped clearing up the bottles from the window sill and sat down opposite him.

Basically, he told me that I'd put him in a really difficult situation last night. Never in a million years had he expected me to ask him to marry him. Apparently that's a man's job. Can you believe he said that in this day and age? And anyway, he felt like he ought to say 'Yes' in front of everyone so he did but the answer is 'No'."

"What! Why doesn't he want to marry you? You've lived together for two years now. You own a house together. It doesn't get much more committed than that."

"That's exactly what I said. But he said that marriage is different. He's quite happy the way things are. He doesn't understand what a big expensive day with fancy clothes and a pair of rings changes," I'm trying to remember all of the lame excuses he gave me, "Oh, and he reckons no-one really enjoys their wedding day anyway. His mate John says he'd have had more fun blowing the lot on the dogs than he did on his wedding day."

"Well, I for one, loved every minute of my wedding day," Eliza recalls. "It was the actual marriage afterwards that was our problem. But you two are made for each other."

"I sometimes wonder. He just can't seem to understand that what I want should matter too. He might not want to get married but I do. For me, it would let the world know how much we love each other. I get sick of talking about 'My boyfriend' at work. It makes me sound like a teenager. When I say 'My partner', I worry they'll think I'm a lesbian."

I can see Eliza laughing at me and I smile without meaning to, "I'm serious. I long for the day I can introduce Dan to someone and say, 'This is Dan, my husband'."

"It does sound like he's being selfish, I have to say, Vicky. I mean where do you go from there? Can you go back to the way things were? How did you leave it with him?"

"Well, that's the thing, you see." Here goes, "He was so adamant that he wasn't going to get married that I got scared and worried that he would call the whole thing off between us. That would be just too awful to think about. Could you imagine having to tell everyone who was here last night that we weren't together any more let alone engaged? And that's when it just came out."

"What have you done, Vicky?" I think Eliza is more on my wave length now.

"It was when he said that we could just pretend I was really drunk last night and it was all just a bit of a joke. I couldn't bare the humiliation of that Eliza, you know me, don't you?"

"Vicky?" she sounds really worried now.

Here goes, "I told him I'm pregnant."

Please say something, Eliza, I'm begging you.

"Oh, my God! I thought you were going to say something awful, you daft cow. That's fantastic! Congratulations. But you shouldn't be drinking that," I can't believe she's grabbing my wine glass off me. She clearly hasn't quite got it yet. "So that's why he looked like the cat that got the cream on the way to the pub."

The whole truth and nothing but the truth, "But I'm not pregnant, Eliza, I made it up."

This silence is so much longer and more torturous than the last one.

"Oh shit." Is that all you've got Eliza? I need more help than that.

I am so ashamed to be telling her this, "I didn't mean to say it. It just kind of, came out. I suppose I was desperate. Dan was absolutely delighted and asked why I didn't just say that in the first place. I made up some crap excuse about wanting to do things in the right order - ha ha - and he said that in that case, we'd definitely get married. Just a small affair, mind, because that's all we can afford this year and it would have to be this year because we'd have to be married before the baby is born, blah, blah, blah."

That feels better. For now anyway.

"He's even rang his mum and dad to tell them the 'happy' news. They've invited us over for a celebratory lunch tomorrow. What have I done Eliza?"

"Wow. I didn't see that one coming. I guess it's not about what you've done but what you're going to do now, honey. We need to think fast tonight."

I knew Eliza wouldn't judge me or hate me. Life is so much easier to face when someone is unconditionally on your side.

"As I see it, you have three options."

"Go on," that's three more than I thought I had.

"Well, you could come clean and tell the truth. I wouldn't hold out much hope for your future as a couple though. He'd never trust you again. But at least you'd be free of the burden of such a huge lie."

"I can't live without him or with the embarrassment of coming clean about what I've done. It was hard enough telling you," I could never repeat my confession to another living soul, "What else can I do?"

"You could go along with the idea for a while then fake a miscarriage."

It's not a pleasant option but worth consideration.

"Or failing that, have you thought about actually having a baby?"

"What?" I can't believe what she's suggesting. Babies are not in my plan for a long time yet.

"It's not so ridiculous, Vicky, you're great with my kids. You'd make a good mum. You must have thought about starting a family one day? You're no spring chicken."

"Well, yes, but not yet. I've got too much living to do first. I want to do better at work and see more of the world before any of that nonsense." Could you imagine me at Barbara's toddler group in that smelly village hall? Or gossiping in the playground about who's knocking off the Butcher?

"It seems to me, you haven't got a lot of options, honey."

She's right, you know, as always. None of these solutions are perfect but all I know is I can't lose Dan or my home. And if it means getting my wedding day after all, it's a price I might have to pay.

"I know you too well to know you won't come clean so you need to just go along with the whole pregnancy thing for now. But you're going to have to act quick if you're going to see it through and actually have a baby."

"What do you mean?"

"Well, only elephants gestate for two years."

"Eh?"

"Feasibly you could be a week or two out with your dates and I know my kids were all born well after their due date. So you'd have to get working at it as soon as possible, if you know what I mean," Eliza has always had a way of making me laugh when she winks at me.

I'm getting the idea, "So I need to get pregnant now."

"Or pretend you are and fake a miscarriage. Either way you've got some serious thinking to do, honey. Wash your wine glass up and put it away because either way, Dan won't want to think you've done half a bottle with me tonight and he'll be back shortly. Right. I'm going to get a taxi booked and get home for my sister - she's been watching the kids. Ring me tomorrow after the lunch thing. Keep your chin up. Remember, you are a newly engaged, pregnant lady, who will be getting married. Smile."

Yet again, Eliza has made things better. Her words and her hugs are the bandages of my life. Being a mum hasn't ruined her life and if I was half as good at it as she is, I'd be okay, wouldn't I?

NELL

I can't believe it's three o'clock in the morning. For all the lights are dimmed, there is no real rest to be had in here. If I had a pound for every time that hideous woman opposite me has rung her bell tonight, all our money problems would be solved. There she goes again. She's got the nurses buzzing around like flies on dog shit. I'm sure I heard her say she's only in here with gastric flu. Crikey, now Snorer's started again next door. I swear I thought only men could make that kind of noise when they slept. If only they hadn't done my D and C so late last night, I think I'd be home in my own, comfy, quiet bed by now. I was so disappointed when they said that I might as well stay to get some rest and go home in the morning. I just despise these places. I'll probably go home more poorly than I arrived if all of those stories in the press about hospital superbugs are to be believed.

Mind you, I don't think I could sleep any better at home anyway. Apart from the circus in here, I can't help going over my phone call to Ric earlier on. It took so long for anyone to get hold of him. He mustn't have been in contact with Rachel at all because I got the message that Rosie was tucked up in Rachel's spare bed when I came back up to the ward, about half past seven.

That's not like Ric. He always rings my mobile to say goodnight to her when he's cooking all evening. And if he knew what was going on, he'd have been straight to pick her up. I reckon it must have been about eight when I checked my phone again and there was nothing.

What I can't stop thinking about - and maybe it's just me going stir crazy in here - is that when I eventually got through to him, on the pay phone the nurse wheeled through, it was Jeanette who answered. Why would she be answering his phone? Surely she'd be busy serving out in the restaurant rather than in the kitchen where Ric keeps his stuff? I don't know. Maybe she had to step in and help wash dishes or something and he asked her to get it while he was busy. She does always seem keen to please, when I've seen her.

But then when I re-play it over in my head, as she passed the phone over to Ric, I couldn't hear the usual background noise of the restaurant: the brash Italian music and the chattering of the diners. And Ric seemed to be there really quickly, like he'd grabbed the phone off her or something. And come to think of it, there were no kitchen noises either. Usually it's hard to hear him above the clattering of pans and shouting of orders. But tonight, he was really clear and I was able to tell him everything without repeating myself. It was all far too quiet.

I hate the road down which this dark, paranoia is taking me. He wouldn't, would he? Jeanette's just a girl. She's in her final year at Uni so she can't be more than about twenty, I suppose. Didn't stop him with that young waitress last time though. I was so stupid back then. I still can't believe I didn't see that one coming. All of those late nights and extra shifts he was 'working' when old Fabio owned the restaurant, which all fitted into place once I found out. I still feel sick when I think about her 'girly chats' every time I went in. I swore I'd never be humiliated like that again.

But I suppose that was before we were married and had Rosie and I truly believed him when he promised it would never happen again. He can't be up to old tricks again. Why is my mind doing this to me? No-one would be that cruel after what's happened the last few weeks.

Maybe that's why he's done it. Because I've been so miserable. Let's face it, I haven't been much fun to be around, physically or emotionally. But then, who would be? He should've been there for me, *in sickness and in health, for better for worse* and all that, not running around after young girls who flutter their eyes at him.

Listen to me, I'm thinking like he's already done something wrong when I've got no real proof, only suspicions. I've got to concentrate on getting some rest, getting better and getting out of here.

Ric did come to the hospital eventually, I suppose, and when the nurses said he really must go, he promised he'll be here first thing in the morning to collect me and this will all be a middle-of-the-night blur. After all, he did apologise for being off radar. I was right, he'd been at the suppliers and I can totally understand how, after that, the Valentine's rush had been so busy he'd lost track of time. I'm doing him a disservice thinking he'd have time to be up to no good, poor man. He works so hard for us. I think it was best to leave all the gory details of my operation until tomorrow. He'd only worry.

Perhaps reading these leaflets the nurse left for me will send me off to sleep. I'm glad they gave me general anaesthetic because I don't think I'd have wanted to go through that awake, even if I couldn't feel anything. At least I know my foetus had already passed and it was just the rest of the conception tissue they were removing. Imagine the poor women who have to watch a doctor take that out. It was bad enough seeing it in private. I wonder what they do with it.

I never did tell Ric that I buried ours in the garden under a rose bush. I felt a bit silly but at the time, it felt like the right thing to do. Every Spring, when those beautiful flowers blossom, I'll remember. I'll remember my baby who was never meant to be, who was too good for us down here and went straight back up to Heaven.

What's this bit on the back of the leaflet? *Rare risks and complications.* The nurse didn't mention much about this. It sounds quite scary: 'weakening of the cervix ... puncturing and scarring of the uterus ... possible infertility'. I know it says 'rare' but it must have happened to someone for them to bother putting it on the leaflet. What if they've damaged me and I can't have any more children?

I mean, I know I've been afraid of going through all this again and I was half thinking we should just call it a day and content ourselves with Rosie. But if the option was taken out of my hands? I don't think I could bear being infertile. I grew up an only child and I know they say that you don't miss what you never had but I don't want that for Rosie. I must give her a play mate, a sparring partner. I do want another baby. Definitely. I know they say to wait a couple of menstrual cycles but what would be the harm in trying before then? I hope and pray that I haven't suffered any damage today and that everything is in good working order.

I must ask the nurse more about it. I'll wait until the morning though or I'll end up just as bad as Moaning Minnie over there. For now, I'll get some sleep before Ric brings my little ray of sunshine to me in the morning.

SHANNON

So this is my new 'ome now then. It's not perfect but anythin's gotta be better than livin' with those two harpin' on at each other. I thought it was just Rob who's a freak but she's just as bad now. She couldn't get my bags packed quick enough this mornin' so that he'd stay. Here's me crappin' myself about tellin' 'em I was comin' to live with Rhys. I thought they'd chuck another bennie but no, it's like, okay, Shannon, that's probably for the best. I'll miss Jack really badly though. It'll be proper weird when he's not jumpin' on my bed to wake me up in the mornin'. I hope they'll be alright with me if I go round to see him now and again. I won't be goin' round to see *them* though, that's for certain. I've 'ad it with them. From now on, Rhys is my family. Jus' me and 'im.

It'll be a bit like bein' on 'oliday really, except without sunny weather and bein' off school. But the rain on the roof window an' the smell of the gas being lit in the kitchen bit is jus' like when we went to Carmarthen Bay with Gran that time.

An' after all, it's dead nice of Rhys's mam to let us 'ave the caravan in the garden. I mean I totally understand when she said there wasn't room to swing a cat in 'er 'ouse and what did we think she was the Salvation Bloody Army. There are a lot o' them like. I didn't know 'er fella an' 'is kids was livin' there too. She did say I wasn't to mention that to anyone though. As far as anyone else needs know, she said pointin' 'er finger at me, they're just over visitin' for the day. Now 'is kids can 'ave Rhys's room on weekends instead of sleepin' bags in the front room. They're all dead nice though. Thomas, the one in Year 11, carried my bag in and put a bog roll in the caravan loo for me. And 'is mam told me to tell 'er if I get any shit off Suzie the slag from the chippy 'cos 'er best mate's husband was shaggin' 'er last year too.

Actually it's well sick bein' in 'ere instead of a house 'cos we can come in any time we want, eat what we want and there'll be no-one to make us tidy up or anythin'. It'll feel well grown up sleepin' in the same bed as Rhys. We'll defo be doin' it now. Can't wait to tell my mates about this on Monday. It's a shame I couldn't carry my laptop as well as all my bags and I'm buggered if I'm goin' back for it yet. I can't even text anyone or nothin' 'cos I 'aven't got any money to get any credit.

Oh well, Rhys'll be back from work soon. I 'ope they were alright with 'im for bein' late this mornin'. Once he tells 'em he was rescuin' his girlfriend from the worst parents in the entire universe, I'm sure they'll understand. Think he finishes at four today so he shouldn't be long now. Best not be 'cos I've read all the *Bella* magazine Rhys's mam gave me. There sure is some shit in there. I can't believe how weird some people's families are. Especially the one where that mam and daughter fell out and didn't speak for like twenty years or somethin'. How stupid is that? I'll never do that to my daughter when I 'ave one. And that woman who chucked 'er son out on the streets to live like a tramp 'cos he'd done a bit of weed or somethin'. Some grown ups are so unreasonable. As Howden says in assembly, we've all got to do a bit of forgivin' and forgettin'.

I suppose I could make a cup of tea or somethin' with that kettle in the kitchen. It looks a bit mingin', especially on the inside. What's that furry stuff at the bottom? Best not to look at that too closely. Doesn't boilin' water kill germs or somethin'? I'm sure I saw some teabags in one o' the cupboards when I was havin' a poke around earlier. There we go. Ooh, half a packet of digestives too. Yuck, they're a bit soggy. I'll leave them 'til my tea's ready and dunk them. Then they'll be soggy anyway. This is the life. Right. Where's the milk? Fridge, where are you? Ah, there's nothin' in it. It's turned off anyway. And there's no plug on the end of the wire. Don't suppose they'd keep milk in 'ere anyway really. Rhys's mam did say it was two long years since they'd managed to get this monstrosity away for an 'oliday.

It's not a monstrosity really. From the outside, it does look a bit mashed up. But once those bricks are taken away and the wheels are put back on, it'll be more on a level. You don't even really notice it from inside. Except when you're on the loo. That felt well weird when I went earlier on. Maybe I could ask Rhys's mam for some cleaning stuff actually 'cos I don't think it's been done since the two long years ago when they had an 'oliday. Rhys said 'is mam sends 'er fella out here for a shit when he's had a curry too. You can tell.

And everythin' else is alright. The nets at the windows give us a bit o' privacy an' the sofa's all squashy so we'll be nice and cosy when we sit down to watch telly. Rhys says he can fix that by bendin' a coat hanger for an aerial. His mam's bringin' some beddin' over later and she said not to look at the mattresses until she does, so I've not been in there yet.

This black tea's a bit funny like but it'll 'ave to do. I don't feel like I can go an' ask for any milk, since they've been so kind to me already. I suppose I could go down the shops and get some. But then I'd run the risk of seeing fake bake chippy slag and being forced to smash 'er face in. An' anyway, I haven't got no money. Hope Rhys's got some or we'll not get any tea. His mam said that if we was livin' independent we'd have to cook independent. I think she was jokin' when she said we'd last a week. We'll be fine in here. Just as long as Rhys goes down for the chips.

SARAH

Dear Lord,

I know it's been a long time since I've spoken to you like this but I can't wait until church tomorrow morning and I really need your help and guidance.

I knew, as soon as I saw her on the doorstep yesterday afternoon, who she was. Call it a lucky guess or instinct, I just knew. She looks a bit like me too, so maybe that was it. She didn't have to ask whether she'd found the right person either because, as we both stood, frozen to the earth beneath us, she simply clarified, 'Sarah Brown?'.

I nodded, glanced back to make sure Tim had driven out of the street, walked past her and opened the door. We both stepped into the hallway and there was silence. There was so much for both of us to say and yet neither of us knew where to start.

"I'm Ellie," she finally declared.

"Oh, I always wondered what they ..." I mumbled back.

"Do you know who I am?"

I nodded again. Of course I knew. She couldn't be anyone else. In a strange kind of way, this young woman didn't look all that different to the last time I'd seen her. The seeds of that dark, tightly curled hair had already been sewn and her blue, almond eyes had only darkened in colour over the years. In all my dreams, this is exactly what she'd looked like. Perhaps the manifestation was even more beautiful than my visions.

"Yes I do," I glanced up at the ceiling to avoid the tears which were welling in my heart. Lord, I had waited for this moment for so long, scripted it in my imagination even. And now it had come, I didn't know what to say. "But I always thought that if you wanted to find me, an agency would contact me first. I'm shocked, I suppose. Listen to me babbling. I just don't know what to say first. How are you? Even that sounds silly. You must have so many questions ..." I stopped there for fear of her thinking I was a complete idiot. All I wanted to do was wrap my arms around her and never let her go again.

With clearly a lot less emotion than I was feeling, she replied, "I managed to avoid all that red tape by getting your details off the computer when the Liaison Officer went out of the room for a moment. After that, a bit of internet searching wasn't difficult. You can find anyone you want these days."

"Well, you'd better come in," I managed and took her through to the lounge. We sat down and I got a closer look at her small flat ears and dimpled chin, neither of which have changed since the day I'd imprinted them on my memory either. I remember weeping as they finally took her from me, telling me that a lovely, young couple were all lined up give her a wonderful life because they weren't fortunate enough to be able to have their own children. How ironic Life can be that eighteen years later, I am that woman who can't seem to have a family of my own. And here, sitting in front of me, was my one shot, my one chance to be a mother, which I gave away to a stranger. She is the sin for which I have been cursed and punished all my married life.

"What it is," Ellie spoke in a in a very matter-of-fact, determined way. She reminded me of myself at a similar age, when I told my parents of my plight and how I would be able to 'get rid of it' if they took me down to a clinic the nurse had recommended. I was unsuccessful in my plan, as they told me that under no circumstances would a good Catholic girl be involved in such murderous activity. No, we would not talk about it again and provision would be made for the child when the time arrived. That, Lord, was the beginning of my dark days. I could not understand how a loving God would want to see such misery and suffering. And as you know, it took me a long time to come back to you and repent of my deeds.

"What it is," she repeated and I could see that she had come here with an agenda much more than just meeting her birth mother, "is that, well, I'm looking for my siblings. I would like to meet the family you went on to have."

"Oh," I was puzzled at this stage and couldn't see what could possibly be more important than explaining why I was forced to give her away. "I, er, never had any more children, Ellie," I confessed.

The disappointment in her face was obvious and I tried hard to understand why, "But I have to say, I'm so glad you tracked me down. You've no idea how much I've always prayed you'd come to find me when you were old enough," I blurted out.

"Well, there you go. I'm here. This is me," she mustered half a smile and her young age was revealed with her sudden change of heart, "But I won't trouble you any longer. I'll be off." With that, she gathered her bag from the floor and headed for the door.

"Won't you stay a bit longer and tell me a bit more about yourself?" I pleaded, "I mean it seems a shame that you went to all this effort for ten minutes."

I could see that this was not how Ellie had rehearsed our moment either. She, too, was no longer the stoic girl that had introduced herself ten minutes earlier. Rather she was becoming increasingly tearful. With all my heart, I wanted to throw my arms around my baby girl and make her see how much I'd missed her, how much I'd regretted letting them take her away from me and most of all, how much I'd thought about her every moment of every day of the last eighteen years.

But I knew I'd foregone that privilege a long time ago. After all, how was a teenager to understand the pressure I'd been under and what life would have been like for me had I chosen to defy my parents? For all my regrets, I had been given no alternative. And when the day came, and the love a mother has for her newborn child was thrust upon me, I knew that I only had one option. How could I subject this heavenly being to a life of struggle with a single parent, who was all but a child herself, when there were people who could provide all that she deserved. Immediately, I loved her too much.

Lord, if this wasn't difficult enough, what Ellie said next will remain with me forever. She faced me and looked me straight in the eye and said, "Well, if I don't have any brothers or sisters, then there's no point in hanging around. I'm done for. It's hopeless."

"Nothing is ever hopeless, Ellie, what do you mean?" I tried to calm her growing anxiety.

She laughed at me. "What would you know?" she retorted, "Have you ever stared at death down the barrel of a loaded gun?"

There was no leaving after that. So we went back into the lounge, sat down again and Ellie composed herself. She explained that she is ill.

"I've got Chronic myelogeneous leukaemia," she began, "which means that I have an increase of white blood cells which.."

"I know," I couldn't help but halt the agonising explanation, "I'm a nurse. Well, a midwife, these days." My angel, who has only just returned, could fly away forever. How much must I be punished, Heavenly Father? Have I not confessed of my sins, repented and praised you? What else did I need to do to stop this torture?

When Ellie explained that she has been taking the drug imatinib but now the resistance drugs are not working properly, it felt like the room had started spinning. My world had been turned upside down twice in such a short time. From what I can gather, a bone marrow transplant from a compatible donor is Ellie's only real hope. I, too, had read the recent statistic she quoted that only 6% of donors are of ethnic origin in Britain, so I can understand how Ellie came to the conclusion that she must find her natural siblings.

"I thought the Liaison Officer said you got married. How come you've not had any more kids yet?" Ellie's words pierced my heart until it felt like the blood was drained.

"Well, you see, the thing is," I began, "I have a syndrome which makes it incredibly difficult to conceive. I didn't know anything about it when I had you. You must have been a blessing from above. So by the time we got married and started to really think about it .. Well, it's just not happened for us."

"But it's not impossible, right?" Ellie enthused, "I mean, they've not said you can never have children."

"No, but, well, we've decided to concentrate on ourselves," articulating our new ethos to someone who was fighting for life, seemed lazy and pathetic. I might as well have said, "We have given up".

"Oh," Ellie sighed, "Didn't you try to get any medical help to have a baby?"

I could see where Ellie was going with this and did everything in my power to divert the conversation but I know she's suggesting that a child of mine, a sibling donor, would be her best chance of survival. I eventually persuaded her to come back to see me on Sunday, before Tim gets back. But before then, I have some serious soul searching to do, Lord. Tim doesn't know about everything from my past. And now that we've decided to stop trying for a child, how could I convince him to start again? That's assuming I want to go ahead and try to have a child to help Ellie myself. I have no idea what I want to do. Please, Heavenly Father, show me the way and guide me at this testing time.

Amen.

HENRY

Unlike Jiya, when I was Henry, I lived until the end of my natural days, albeit in the most unnatural of circumstances. I went to sleep one night, with no more than the usual frailty of an elderly man, and simply didn't wake up. No fear, no knowledge of the inevitable but a peaceful passing, and perhaps, a smile that things were looking up.

As I lay on my age-flattened, rough wool mat that very night, I wondered if, indeed, that this would be the last day my mealie and bread would be rationed. The possibility that I would no longer be made to feel grateful that it was more than my Bantus friends received, or feel ashamed when I was given the portion of jam that they were denied, filled me with a warmth that invaded my entire body.

Rumours had been spreading like a virus over the last few months of my life. Of course, no one ever knew how true they were; one heavily censored letter every six months did not constitute accurate communication with the reality of the outside world. But, like any other virus, it had found a way of infiltrating, no matter how hard the guards tried to stop it. First we'd heard that FW de Klerk had finally relaxed the apartheid laws, then that our great leader had been released from Victor Verster and now, they were saying that the prison was to be closed forever.

Now, I had lived a long enough life to learn the bitter disappointment of having your hopes and dreams raised, only to be slammed back down to where they belong. But somehow, this seemed different. The wind had changed and it seemed that our work was eventually done. Obviously, I didn't know quite how little time I had left on Earth but I told myself that night, that the rest of my days would be spent in a different world. A world where freedom and equality would finally emerge, singing the anthems of those of us who had spent our lives struggling and fighting.

In a funny kind of way, I prayed for the kind of freedom we had possessed when I was growing up in District Six, where merchants lived alongside former slaves and coloureds mixed happily with their Indian neighbours. Of course, this rainbow jigsaw was smashed apart the moment the government decided we were all dangerous criminals and prostitutes, drinking and gambling our lives away. The individual pieces were to be sorted and put into piles, never to risk reconnection again.

I never forgot the humiliation in my mother's eyes when she was forced to test her hair with a pencil to see which type of

African she really was, or the tears in my wife's eyes, when they bulldozed the house we had only just begun to set up as a newly married couple. Looking back, I suppose these were the catalysts which provoked me into joining the ANC and making my voice heard.

I had been told that there was soon to be a peaceful protest against the dompas, as we called it. But when the word spread, on that fateful day, that the PAC were starting the protest early, in Sharpeville, I cared not to which group I belonged or whether they were peaceful. I thought of my mother and my wife and how much I hated carrying around that stupid dompas, the supposed proof of my right to work in the country where I had lived all my life.

That was the day, in the eyes of the law, that I became a criminal. I dared not tell Elizabeth where I was going, for I knew she would try to persuade me that it was a bad idea. When I arrived, Sharpeville was busier than I'd ever seen it before. People gathered on the roads and at first, many were simply singing, dancing and chanting. When we offered ourselves to the police, for not carrying our cards, I could see the surprise and fear in their eyes. Clearly, they had not expected so many to turn up. We outnumbered the police officers by hundreds, if not thousands, and so the balance of power was tipped and it ignited the inferno which was to follow.

Despite the police officers' best attempts, they could not regain control of the township and so our stone throwing was greeted with firearms. Every African that fell to the ground that day was ammunition to be stored up for later use. Feeling lucky not to be one of those shot down, I fled back home to Elizabeth. But I had seen familiar faces in the crowds and knew that I would have been spotted too. Our next ANC meeting would be dangerous.

When, that night, Elizabeth told me that I was to become a father, my head told me that my involvement in the riot had been reckless and that my priority should be my expanding family. But my heart told me that now, more than ever, I should fight for the future of my unborn child. How could I bring another life into this world of oppression and inequality? Surely this new human being was made of the same fabric as any other on the planet and deserved exactly the same opportunities?

Now banned, the meetings had to be organised in the utmost secrecy and I went several times, at nightfall, to hear our leaders plan the next demonstrations. It was one such night that I was arrested and charged with killing a young police officer. I knew nothing of the accusation, but in my heart, could not truly deny that this had not been the case. In my rage in Sharpeville, anything was possible. I had become an animal that day and could well have committed crimes beyond my control.

The journey across to Robben Island was bleak. Not only was I about to join the ghosts of lepers and outcasts who had been left there to rot centuries before, but the wind lashed through my flesh, trying to whip out my soul.

Unbeaten, the first few years of my incarceration were the most informative of my life. Of course, there were troubles in the prison; sixty men in a cell made for twenty was overcrowded to say the least. And to make things worse, this was one place where segregation was not enforced. Men from very different ideologies did not always see eye to eye and violent fights sometimes broke out. But what we lost in our basic rights as human beings, we gained in knowledge. Having previously held only a hatred of apartheid and a passion for justice, I came to possess a sound understanding of politics and discovered a talent for rhetoric. I used this to produce material which managed to find its way to our new generation of followers on the outside.

Over the years, learning sharpened my mind and digging in the quarry strengthened my body. Oh, the hours we spent digging for limestone. The dust made us cough and the relentless sun beat down on our bodies and glared from the white rock into our eyes. It was only clinging on to the thought of progress for Africa which retained my sanity. In my moments of weakness, when I thought about Elizabeth, and the child I never met, I focused on all of the wives, mothers and children of our country and how my life could be used to make things better for them.

And so all these years later, lying in the small cell I now inhabited on my own, I felt a sense of pride that my pamphlets and leaflets may have played some part in the changing world. And then a strange feeling came over me. The wind may have been changing outside, but for me, inside, it seemed to stop. The very breath that had served me for all these years ceased to flow. In the same way that a new born baby knows instinctively how to be born, I let myself go. Finally, I was free.

VICKY

What a weekend. I can't believe how significantly my life has changed in just a couple of days. I mean, I knew that it would be a fantastic weekend after the party and us getting engaged but this isn't quite how I thought it would pan out. My head is spinning and I'm finding it all just a bit overwhelming. I think this 'pregnancy' thing is going to be useful. Dan didn't flicker when I said I didn't have the energy to do the usual Sunday night shirt ironing routine and needed to come up here for a soak in the bath instead. What bliss.

I shouldn't joke about it, really. I've got myself into a right old situation and Eliza is so right. I've got to act fast. Last night, her 'miscarriage' idea was the perfect solution. No-one would find out that I'd lied and Dan would feel so dreadful when it 'happened' that he wouldn't be able to go back on agreeing to marry me. Win, win.

But after today, I'm not so sure. Dan was so lovely this morning when brought me breakfast in bed. And when he stayed at home to read the newspapers with me rather than have his Sunday morning pint over the road, I felt like a real princess. I did get the feeling he was actually pleased about this 'baby'.

Reality hit though when we went round to Dan's parents for Sunday lunch. I couldn't believe that even Emma and Tom managed a smile or two when they were all congratulating us. I mean, I know I'm not one for standing in the limelight or anything, but it was lovely to have everyone fussing over me. A tear came to my eye when Dan's dad gave up his special chair for me and said I'd better sit down in 'Grandad's chair'. Bless him, he's so excited already. With all the chatter about due dates and baby names, I almost forgot the fiction of it all and started to believe it myself.

It was when Dan's mum brought out his baby photos that it started to feel a bit awkward. They all sat cooing and reminiscing about what little hair Dan had for such a long time and the way he gave a really cheesy thumbs up on every photo taken during his childhood. Dan got all defensive and deflected the laughter on to his mum when he told them how awful the jumpers were that she'd knitted for him every year. That was all well and good but when his mum said, 'You've got all this to come, Vicky, with our new little Dan' and his Dad added, 'Or Daniella' I began to feel such shame.

Already, in their eyes, they have added a branch to their family tree. The seed has been sewn and their name, genetic make up and lack of hair will be passed on to another generation. And here I am, about to rip it all away from them. I mean I know miscarriages can happen but I can tell they'd be devastated already if they lost the grandchild they've clearly been dreaming of for years.

When they finally went up into the loft to retrieve that ghastly reindeer jumper from Dan's second Christmas, and brought down the family Christening gown for 'a good wash', in case we might want to use it, I knew I had to leave. I suppose it was about three o'clock anyway and I knew Dan wouldn't mind getting back for that pint he'd missed this morning.

One way or another, I'm going to have to ring and tell Mum this week because when they were clearing the lunch dishes, I overheard Dan's dad say that at least this would be something to write about in the card this year. I'm not sure why, but they insist on writing letters in the Easter cards they send to Mum. It's quite sweet really, I suppose but I can't let that be the first she hears about it.

My conversation with Mum will be the hardest so far. I can't be truthful with her, like I was with Eliza. She'd be absolutely disgusted at my deceit. Plus, I can't burden her with worry, over there on her own. I know she professes that moving over to Spain was the best thing she's done since Dad died but I can tell it's not everything that she imagined. She's far too proud to admit it but I know. I guess, that in the same way, she'll sense that I'm not entirely telling the truth about the baby. I can't explain it but there's just this unspoken truth with Mum. It's like, I can tell within nano-seconds of a conversation whether she's tired, unwell, worried or unhappy. I'm not stupid enough to think she doesn't read me in the same way too.

At least Maggie will save me the job of telling everyone in Freddock. She was so funny in the shop this afternoon. As soon as I saw her, I knew she was bursting to say something so I let her slowly simmer as she chatted about her Amateur Dramatics play this Spring and tried to persuade me that there was a perfect part left for me: a beautiful, popular, successful career girl or something.

"But I hear you might be too, shall we say, rotund, by May!" she boiled over, "Oh, I'm sorry, Dan swore me to secrecy last night in the pub but I just can't help myself. I'm so happy for you both. It won't be long before you'll be shouting it from the rooftops yourselves anyway," she justified. I guess I'll be the hot topic of village gossip this week then. Well, at least I'll be talked about. What is it they say? *It's better to be talked about than not talked about at all.*

I can just imagine the next Summer Fair Committee meeting. No more tea bag debate. It'll be all about our baby. Barbara and Frances will be enlisting me in their toddler groups, buggy hikes and all sorts. Old Norman will be testing the ground for whether we'll be having a Christening and subtly hinting that it might be better to start coming to church on a Sunday sooner rather than later.

I'd never really thought about it but people are much more excited by the prospect of a baby than by a wedding. Neither Maggie nor Dan's parents said much about the wedding at all. I imagined that everyone would want to know all about our grand plans but it seems that's all paled into insignificance now.

I've only got myself to blame. What a tangled web I've woven. I've got my fiancé, of course, and I can't wait to refer to Dan as such tomorrow at work. There's no way that can change now. He's doing the right thing and marrying me and I actually believe he's thrilled about having a child together. I wouldn't ruin that by telling the truth. And what harm is my little white lie doing?

Certainly lying again, by saying I lost a baby, would hurt people though. Dan and our families would be really upset and I'd have to go through more difficult pretence. I don't think I could bear it.

That just leaves the option of getting pregnant for real. Once the awkwardness of my fake-pregnancy is over, I could really enjoy the attention of it all, you know. I've done the hard part now, I guess. No-one thought that me becoming a parent was a terrible idea, or at least they didn't say so. They must think I'm up to it. And I think I am.

It wouldn't be so bad. How hard can it be? Eliza's right. I do like her kids and I'd adore my own flesh and blood. And if she's managed alone for all these years, Dan and I can do it together, with the support of our family and friends. Hey, it might even be a good enough reason for Mum to come back from Spain. We're alright financially and plenty of women pick their careers up again after they've been off on maternity leave. Freddock can be a bit dull at times, but it's the perfect place to have a child. I never had all this green, open space when I was growing up but I can see how good and safe it is for all the children in the village. And Maggie's always telling me about families who move here to get into the school. Half the world's involved in this child rearing business. There must be something in it.

Our child would be safe, loved and wanted from the start. Did I say 'would'? I mean 'will'. Rather than a problem to be solved, this as an opportunity to begin the next chapter of our lives together. I'm ready. I just need one vital ingredient to pull this plan together. I've got some baby-making to organise.

NELL

Hello Mum,

I hope you like these snowdrops. Rosie picked them out of our garden for me when I got back from the hospital at lunchtime. The daffodils will be out soon but there's not much else growing yet. Still, you always loved the snowdrops, didn't you? First sign that Spring is on its way, you used to tell me when I was little, shows that Mother Nature is beginning her new year.

Well, our new start isn't in sight yet, Mum. I hoped the new baby would give us something to look forward to, to distract us from conversations about bills, overdrafts and business loans. It's all we seem to talk about these days. Business is dreadful. But it wasn't the only reason. I longed for Rosie to have the brother or sister that you could never give me. I wanted her to have someone to turn to when she grew up, someone to rely on for unconditional love and support when times were rough, even just someone whose house she could go to for coffee, when she fancied a chat. But it wasn't meant to be.

Please look after my fledgling angel. Teach him to fly and to love and tell him that I wanted him so much. Let me feel that he's not too far away and is smiling down on me, like I feel you sometimes, Mum.

I needed to get out by myself this afternoon, to talk to you and to get my head straight. As if things hadn't been bad enough with the miscarriage and being in hospital, I'm worried about Ric. Well, not so much worried about him but worried about what he's been up to. When I couldn't contact him in the hospital, I felt so alone and so scared. I missed you more than ever and knew that you'd have been there for me right away. But not Ric. I just can't rely on him any more, Mum. He managed to convince me that he'd been at the suppliers' and had no signal which satisfied my suspicions and I did manage a few hours' sleep after that.

Then this morning, when I woke, all I could think about was seeing my Rosie, my one constant in this ever changing life. She's so beautiful, Mum. I wish you could have met her. She has Ric's dark hair and skin but when she looks at me, it's your deep blue eyes I can see. *Laughing eyes*, people used to say. But he didn't bring her to the hospital.

"Where is she?" I demanded as soon as I saw Ric walk into the ward.

"Hello to you too, Nelly," he smoothed and kissed my head.

"Where's Rosie?" I asked him again.

"Ah, I left her playing at home with Jeanette. They were were playing with, how you say? *Play Doh*."

My heart bounced in my chest and a chill cascaded from my skull to my feet. Jeanette's his waitress, Mum, and she's never been to our house before. I'd had a fleeting suspicion about them the night before when she'd answered his mobile but then I'd convinced myself that I was just being stupid after a long, tiring day.

"Jeanette?" I spat out, "What's she doing at our house?"

"Just a spot of babysitting. What's the use of staff if you don't employ them, huh? Anyway, more importantly, how are you my sweet love? Have they been looking after you?"

And that was it, brushed over. He'd managed yet again to avoid the conversation I wanted to have and make me feel stupid for pursuing it any further. That's the way he's been about the miscarriage too. Every time I broach the subject, he changes it and makes some flippant remark. I swear he's pleased it didn't work out. And now I know why. He's been sleeping with that little whore.

I got my last piece of proof when I got home. As soon as I walked in the door, Jeanette passed Rosie to me and rambled something about having to dash off. I swear she couldn't look me in the eye and I just knew something wasn't right. Ric went to make a cup of tea and I held my daughter more tightly than ever. Knowing someone has wronged you is one thing but accusing them is another. I was teetering on the verge of losing everything. I took a deep breath and went to sit down in the lounge to plan my next step.

And there, staring me in the face was all the evidence I needed. On the windowsill, the three scented candles I bought only a few days ago, but haven't had a chance to use, were burned half way down their wick. Ric has never lit a candle in our house during the entirety of our relationship. He jokes about not having paid the electricity bill every time I light them. I couldn't imagine why Jeanette would have burned the candles on a Sunday morning when she was babysitting a three year old. She must have stayed over and she must have lit them last night. Even my house is telling me that my husband is having an affair.

Filled with the rage of a wild animal, I no longer felt like I needed a game plan. It was over and I needed some answers. But then Rosie broke my red mist.

"Mummy," she said, "Did you bring a baby home from the hospital?"

And my anger was gone, washed away by an increasingly familiar wave of grief.

"No, Rosie, no I didn't. What made you think that?" I asked. I was sure I'd kept her protected her from all that had gone on recently.

"Callum's mummy got one there and Laura's going to hospital to get one for Emily soon," she told me.

Indeed she was right. And, Mum, that's when I knew I couldn't do it. Call me weak or call me selfish but I couldn't explode our little family. We've come this far and I so desperately long for another child. If I end our marriage now, then my dreams are over too. At that moment I realised that I must ignore the glaringly obvious truth and carry on as normal. I need to have that baby and I will. Some stupid little girl, who's caught my husband's eye, isn't going to spoil that for me. She's not going to win. I deserve better.

So I drank my tea and told Ric all about the events of the previous day, and night. If anything, I felt myself laughing and flirting with him, like in the old days, telling him about the bell ringer opposite and the snorer next door. I needed him to notice me, to desire me and, when the time is right, to give me what I want.

Mum, please don't think badly of me. I don't know what you would have done. I realise now that after Dad left, you kept any relationships you might have had hidden away from me, like a dirty secret, for fear of upsetting me, I presume. So I never learned how to work at a marriage or when it was time to quit. But what you did teach me is how to be a good mother and so I'm putting Rosie, and any other children we may be blessed with, first. Who knows what the future may hold but that's what's right for now.

SHANNON

"It's proper amazin' Sian, livin' with your boyfriend.
Dead romantic. No parents to bang on about music or bedtime or
nothin'. We're like a proper couple." Well, I don't want to sound
like I'm braggin' or nothin' but she did ask me.

"Sounds well good. Did you *do it* then?"

"Yeah, course we did. All night."

"Tell us then, what's he like? Was it good?"

Well I'm not about to go into all the gory details here in
the shoppin' centre, especially outside *Poundland*, 'cos there's
loads of people from school hangin' around here and I wouldn't
want to sound like a slapper or anythin'.

"Well good," that's all she's gettin' for now. An' anyway,
what am I supposed to say? A bit crap really? Not like they do it
on telly? All messy and fiddly when we had to put the condom
on? Done and dusted in about two minutes 'cos that was Rhys's
first time too? "I'll message you about it when I get me laptop
back."

"Where is it like?"

"At me mam an' dad's."

"Can't you just go an' get it?"

If only. I've told Sian how mental they are an' how they virtually chucked me out but I can't tell 'er that if I went round I think I'd start to cry and just want to hug my mam forever and never let go or leave the 'ouse again. An' I wouldn't let Rob see that.

"Nah, not really. I'll get Rhys to go round for it soon."

"Where's Rhys today then?"

"He didn't want to come down the precinct so he just stayed at home and went back in the house to watch telly and get a shower and stuff." Hope Sian doesn't realise that we don't have a shower in the caravan. She'll think I'm proper mingin' if she knows I haven't 'ad a wash since I left my 'ouse yesterday mornin'. Rhys was proper mingin' this morning after workin' in the garage all day yesterday and not gettin' washed. I 'ope I don't smell like 'im. Might 'ave to go to *Superdrug* an' 'ave a squirt of body spray in a bit.

"You 'ad lunch yet Shannon?" I thought she'd never ask. I'm starvin'. When Rhys went for the chips las' night, he only 'ad one pound thirty so we 'ad to share a bag an' I've 'ad nothin' else since. Bet he's 'avin' somethin' nice in the 'ouse now though.

"No but I got no money left."

"I've got some. Let's go an' get some sausage rolls."
Sian is the bestest friend ever.

As we walk down the street, I can't 'elp starin' at all the
kids out with their mams, especially the little girls. We used to be
like that once, me and my mam. It was just 'er an' me against the
world. I mean, she was always a bit shouty an' that an' told me
off for stuff but we used to do things together an' nothin' or no-
one else mattered back then. Now I'm not even sure if she loves
me. Rob has changed all that. She's been so desperate to keep
'im the las' few years that he's come first, second and third place.
It's not like he's even good lookin' or nothin'. When she 'ad
Jack, I thought it might change a bit but it jus' made 'er more
tired and stressy 'cos Rob never lifts a finger.

This sausage roll is well nice. I was so hungry . That's
what super models must feel like when they're trying to stay size
zero and mega skinny. Although I don't think they eat many
sausage rolls.

"I'm so jealous of you Shannon, livin' with Rhys. You're
so grown up," Sian confesses to me. "My mam and dad drive me
bonkers 'alf the time. I'd love to live by myself. Can I come
round sometime to see the caravan?"

I've jus' nearly spat out a bit o' my sausage roll, "Maybe," I lie. If Sian saw the shitty state of our tin 'ouse an' felt 'ow cold it is at night an' smelt my stinkin' boyfriend in the mornin' an' 'ad no money an' was starvin' 'alf to death, she'd soon change 'er mind, jus' like I did this mornin'.

"I mean, you're so lucky that Rhys's mam gave you the caravan jus' to live in for free," Sian continues, oblivious that she is talkin' crap.

"S'pose so,"

"'Cos you remember that Chantelle girl in the year above us? The one who 'ad to leave school early before 'er GCSEs? When 'er mam chucked 'er out to live with 'er Gran 'cos she was shopliftin' from *Boots* she 'ad to get up the duff,"

"Oh, yeah, I remember her: ginger, big boobs," I'd forgotten about her. "What d'you mean she *'ad* to get up the duff?"

"Well, to get an 'ouse to live in. She didn't want to live with 'er Gran 'cos she was well harsh so now she lives other side of town now with her little 'un. Matty and 'er split up an' he went back 'ome but she got the flat for keeps."

"How come?"

"Dunno really. Think the government 'ave to give you somewhere to live if you're preggers an' have nowhere to go. My brother's been round hers for a party but he says she never gets out much an' has no money or nothin' so all I'm sayin' is you're well lucky that you got the place for free an' don't 'ave to be stuck with a baby or anythin'."

I can hear Sian dronin' on about that Chantelle girl but my mind is stuck on what she said about the government givin' you an 'ouse if you're pregnant.

Bingo. Sian might think 'avin' a baby's like the worst thing in the entire universe but I've 'ad one for the past two years. I've done everythin' for Jack. Feedin', changin', bathin' an' I loved every minute of it. The only thing I didn't do for 'im was push 'im out my fanny. An' that can't be as horrible as they make out on telly. I mean, my mam's pathetic when she gets a paper cut so she wouldn't 'ave done it twice if it was really bad, would she?

If I can look after Jack, I can 'ave my own kid, no probs. Then me an' Rhys could 'ave a warm place to live, with our own shower an' our own fridge. No more stinkin' caravan an' no more mam an' dad. We'll be well sorted.

SARAH

"So you're going to up to Birmingham University in September?" I'm trying desperately to remember the nuggets of 'normal' information Ellie gave me on Friday, as I pour us some tea. What is it about this little bag of leaves which is so suitable for every circumstance in life? Its comforting properties are equally appropriate for a funeral or a birthday celebration. Nature's embrace, I always think, a hug in a mug. We take our cups and go into the lounge. "Which subject are you reading?"

"Environmental Studies ... if I ever get there," she looks down to the carpet.

This is not going to go well, I can tell. How on Earth can we talk about anything other than the agendas we've both brought to the table today? It is taking me all the self-restraint I possess not to smother her with kisses and tell her how she's made my every dream come true by just being here. I want to sniff her, to see if she still has that heavenly scent I tried so desperately to remember all those years, that addictive smell of your newborn child. I kept it for a while on the little white hat that fell from her precious head when they took her away. But, of course, it faded, just like everything else.

Ellie doesn't want to hear any of this though. She's not here to find her mother, or to tell me about everything I've missed over the last eighteen years. She's just here to find a bunch of cells to make her better. I understand that.

"So how are you feeling, Ellie? I mean, I know you're unwell and all, but generally, how's it making you feel?" Really stupid question, I know but I can't bear the alternative silence.

"Oh, top of the world," Ellie isn't giving me anything today. She was much more open on Friday but I can't unlock her at all today. How can she have belonged to me once upon a time? I carried her in my womb for nine long months and my arms were the first to hold her when she entered the world but now it seems we have absolutely no link left at all, no thread that I always imagined connected us, however far she was away from me. She doesn't seem to want to know anything about me - other than my reproductive plans - or why I had to give her away.

Those almond eyes look at me in the eye for the first time today, "I'll cut to the chase, Sarah."

Calling me by my Christian name is the final twist of the knife. I don't know what I expected. She's had another mother for eighteen years and she's hardly about to call anyone else by that name now, is she? But somehow it matters. In my dreams of us being reunited, she falls into my arms and calls me Mummy immediately, claiming that she always knew her parents weren't really the ones she was meant to be with.

But life's no dream and here we are with the awful reality.

"I need to know if I ever stand a real chance of having a sibling. I know you were really young when you gave birth to me and so, with all due respect, you must still be of an age where it's something you'd consider. And I got the impression you'd had fertility issues the other day but you didn't say it was impossible, did you? Medical technology is amazing these days and there all sorts of things they can do for people like you. But if there's no chance you'd try some fertility treatment and you definitely don't want to have any children, then I won't bother you any more and I'll go back to what's left of my own life."

Don't want any more children? If only she knew what she was saying. If only she knew how hard we'd tried over the last few years and how disappointed we'd been at every negative pregnancy test, then she'd understand. Maybe I'd wanted to replace my first daughter, I don't know, but I'd wanted another baby with Tim, every bit as I'd wanted to keep Ellie in the first place. I know I'd convinced myself, and Tim, that our life is going to be fine without children but we both know deep down that we're just protecting ourselves from any more pain. Sometimes you just have to numb the skin to stop the itch.

"It's just not that simple, Ellie, I'm afraid," I explain but try not to patronise, trying to recognise that she is coping with an illness adults twice her age find difficult to deal with. "Up until recently, very recently in fact, my husband Tim and I have actually been desperately trying but it's just not happening for us. I do know that there's a drug I can have to encourage regular ovulation but the doctor I saw said I'd have to lose a bit more weight first. And that's been difficult too." I feel ashamed to say that last bit, in light of what this poor young girl has had to deal with. "All of that was putting so much pressure on our relationship that we decided to stop trying and enjoy life before it passes us by." Why did I say that? I'm so tactless sometimes. I feel dreadful.

"Well lucky you. Some of us don't have the luxury of watching life pass us by." I can forgive her outright rudeness. In fact, I could forgive anything she said or did. "Why haven't you tried IVF though?"

Here comes the tricky bit. "Well, Ellie, I'm Catholic. I know it may sound stupid to you when all you know about me is that I had a teenage pregnancy, out of wedlock, which certainly isn't very Catholic at all." I don't think my loss of Catholic values, when I wanted to have an abortion, will enhance the story or her opinion of me.

"But I grew up within the Catholic Church and, despite my sins, I found God again later in my life."

"I don't follow. Surely your God would want you to have a baby and be happy. Doesn't he tell you to go forth and multiply or something," Ellie looks confused.

"Yes, that's true," I tell her, "But only in the sanctity of the marital bed, if you know what I mean." For all my years of discussing baby-making processes with my ladies at work, I'm less comfortable than ever, talking about the whole ordeal with Ellie.

"And an IVF child is conceived in a laboratory." She's bright.

"Not only that but the Catholic Church believes that when the sperm fertilises the ovum and an embryo is created, life begins. In IVF, the doctors have to create several more embryos than they need to use and so, to put it brutally, mini-lives are thrown away." I hope that does it justice.

"Couldn't you just ask them to fertilise one and hope that that embryo implants?"

She's right, you know. I'd never thought about that before. Sometimes you get so wrapped up in what is forbidden that you can't see what is possible.

"I'm sorry to put you through explaining all of this but it seems clear to me that you want a baby as much as I want you to have one. Theoretically, where would your Church stand on bone marrow donation, if theoretically, you had another child which was, theoretically, compatible with me?"

"I'm not sure, Ellie, I've never really had to think about it before. I suppose if no-one is harmed in the process," I'm bumbling my way through this conversation now because she's got my head spinning, "but as you pointed out there's a lot of theorising there, love. You've got to realise that there are no guarantees with IVF and no guarantees with marrow matching."

"But it's got to be worth a shot. I'm not trying to persuade you do something that would ruin your life. You obviously want a baby really badly but just haven't found the solution yet. We'd both gain from this, can't you see?" Ellie's passion sweeps me along like a leaf in the wind and I can do nothing more than nod my head. This young girl is sitting in front of me fighting for her life, like I should have fought for her all those years ago. How can I deny her this chance? God and Church aside, I have an opportunity, no an obligation, to put things right and that's what I must do.

KAUFMANN

The further back my memories take me, the more
fragmented they become. Nonetheless, I am transported back to a
series of still images, evoking reveries of yet another life I once
had.

I can see what I know to be myself, sitting in a room.
With my kippah drawing a strong outline for my skull, I look up
to my father who is leading the prayers as we welcome the
Shabbat, in the warm glow of the candles my mother has just lit.

Flooding back, like an evening tide, comes the knowledge
that we would spend every Shabbat in this way, together as a
family, thanking God for our lot. My father worked in a bank and
we had a life, not of luxury, but of plenty. Although the fire had
to remain unlit that night each week, my parents, my siblings and
I sat together in a room which never felt cold.

While my sister played for hours with a lovingly decorated
wooden dolls' house, my brother and I would be equally absorbed
in the tin soldiers my father had brought in for us one day. We
always knew mother didn't really approve but we adored them
just the same. I would divide them up into the four kingdoms and
was always the Prussian Army. My brother never held such

loyalty and switched regularly between the others. Strategies in place and infantry lined up, battle would commence. Bedtime was usually announced when the soldiers began their attack on the dolls' house.

To say that my childhood was uneventful, would be to do it a huge disservice but I remember no monumental occasions which changed the course of the lives of those contented little children.

The next image I have, is of myself much taller and almost a man. I have swapped my kippah for a spiked helmet and look not dissimilar to a life-size manifestation of those tin soldiers. This time my father is watching me, as I place my left hand on the staff of the colours and raise my right hand for God and the Fatherland. My mother and sister are wiping tears of pride and my brother looks on with envy and anticipation that he, too, will soon register to volunteer.

This was what I had waited for all of my childhood. I knew that I was fit and healthy and would certainly pass the physical examination at the muster. But when I stood there before my family, I felt such achievement and importance. The weeks of preparatory drill and discipline were gruelling but had allowed me to prove that I could serve and protect my country, if ever I should be required.

The man I see in the next picture looks so very different and yet I know it is me. I can see that it must not have been too long before my eager contribution was necessary. I remember now, with tender affection, the short time before this picture, in the barracks with my comrades. The Mess was a constant hive of activity and the men with whom I shared a room, became as close to me as my own brother. Food was meagre but it was ample enough reward for our new way of life. We were not Prussian or Bavarian, Saxon or Wuttenberg. I was no longer Jewish nor German. We were Men, waiting to defend our Nation.

But this man is different. Gone is the spark in his eyes; gone is the belief that he will save the Fatherland. He stands, a boy in a man's body and clothes, looking like he would rather be anywhere else on Earth than this hole in the ground somewhere in a foreign land.

I recall hearing that we were better off than the English soldiers. Talk was, that their trenches were not as deep as ours and their lack of military foresight had resulted in a more temporary type of accommodation, without the drainage systems and seating areas, which kept us mostly dry. Furthermore, we'd been here first and built on higher ground which had served to our advantage in the efforts so far. Indeed we had goats for milk and the men said that these new machine guns would keep us safe.

But it was difficult to remain grateful for long. I laughed with my friends at the sound of frying lice, as we picked them from our scalps and dropped them into a shoe polish tin, heated by a candle. But nobody truly thought it was funny and no-one laughed when they were alone and found the little red creatures in their underpants, making an expedition to God knows where and itching like Hell, every inch of their journey.

Rats were another species of trench-mate but despite their size and constant noise, at least they were visible. What we couldn't see coming was the icy cold weather, which threatened our feet as much as any enemy. Men who suffered most watched as their toes, swollen and deformed inside their boots, died on their feet.

The death of a digit was painful but the death of a comrade was worse. I remember distinctly the time I was unfortunate enough to watch this with my own eyes. In the most surreal of our experiences, fighting had ceased on Christmas Day and we all enjoyed a game of football on No Man's Land. Only one day before, we had been taking aim at these men's heads and shooting them down. And now, we were heading the ball to them and shooting past their goalkeeper. I think this joviality had psychologically disarmed us for a moment, because the following day, before we could stop him, Hans jumped over the parapet to readjust some barbed wire which had been disturbed in the previous festivities. And that's when it happened.

His body leapt in the air and descended like a felled tree, until it lay prostate with the ground. We all looked on in horror and fear. Hans lay there for some time, rotting and decaying with the multitudes that no-one would ever make the suicide mission to recover, his corpse a constant reminder that Christmas was over.

As if to buoy our spirits, there was much talk of a new chlorine gas, which would revolutionise warfare, and as far as we knew, we were the first to have it available for use. It would asphyxiate the enemy and result in a slow, painful death.

When a letter came from my sister, and I sat to write my reply, I wanted to tell her of this impending tactic, to reassure her that things were going to be alright. But I knew such information was not allowed to be penned, so instead, I told her of the chilly climate of Northern France and the warmth her letter had sent me. I did, however, think about the chlorine gas when I carefully replaced her letter in the envelope and looked at the stamp. *Gott strafe England,* it read. *Punished they will be*, I agreed, when they breathe in our cloud of chemicals. Feeling stronger than I had in a long time, I waited for our turn to shine, our turn to avenge the death of Hans.

I recall little of the last day of my life. Snippets of orders, shouted at me and the other men, to go over the top once the gas had been released, pervade an otherwise darkening memory. "The wind has changed!" are the last words I heard, in my life as Kaufmann, and I was very soon to realise their significance. The damage I'd hoped to inflict on the enemy was quick to blow back in my face. What had started as a feint whiff of something between pepper and the liquid my mother used to use to clean the kitchen floor, grew stronger and the dirty yellow cloud we'd waved off to the other side, was all I could see. Like an onion, my eyes were peeled of their cells, layer by layer. The harder I tried not to breathe, the more my rasping lungs grabbed for the poisonous air outside. The Devil was eating me alive, starting with my innards. Falling to the ground, I could do no other than face my fate and I prayed that the denser gas down there would speed up the process. Hans had been the lucky one to be shot down in an instant; I lay there for hours writhing in the agony of my death.

I've heard it said that a human being's moment of true enlightenment comes at the moment of their passing. It was at that point that I realised how foolish I had been. To be gunned down or blown up by the enemy is one thing but to fall at your own side's blunder is another. I was no hero. I wasn't going to be eternally honoured by my country for the sacrifice I had made. I was just another tin soldier, knocked over in the game. I would be replaced and forgotten, just as we had done in our childhood play. Never would I get the chance to have my own family and watch them grow, enjoying each Shabbat in our wonderful Fatherland.

ME

Remembering my lives and deaths brings me comfort, knowing that I have lived and loved and seen much of what the human experience has to offer. But I have also known hardship beyond measure, I have lost my freedom and my lives have been wasted because of the actions of others. I do not remember the slugs or the willow trees I surely must have been during my journey, but I can see now that my soul is one of few, fortunate enough to live multiple human lives. The Hindus talk of rebirth, the Buddhists of reincarnation, the ancient Greek philosophers documented such theories and even the Christians believe Jesus will come back again. And now I know it is true. My soul, like a phoenix, will return. This time I know it will have a special purpose and I am certain that this life will be different to those which have gone before. I have come so close to enlightenment and fulfilment in the past but never had opportunities such as these women offer me.

Spending time inside the minds of my potential mothers has shown me who they really are. Of course we can watch others, listen to what they say and judge their actions but we never truly know a person until we walk a day in their shoes. And having done so, I am more shocked than I was before. These self-gratifying lives are unlike any I have lived. None of them appear to know any bounds in their pursuit of personal happiness. They blunder through life with varying degrees of disregard for those closest to them. I am quite certain there is nothing they would not do to achieve their desires.

I cannot ignore the reasons these women want to have a baby. A child should come into this world not only by love but also by honesty and truth. Deceit is an ugly parasite which feeds on all that is beautiful and pure, leaving it marred forever. Furthermore, children are not tools and cannot be used to construct relationships; they will break and disintegrate rather than mend.

Having waited so long for my soul to return to a life where I can prosper and reach my awakening, I cannot begin my days like this, as someone's deepest, darkest secret, created to make something else work. Surely this is not the plan. I cannot see how any of these women can serve my soul well. Indeed, I am fearful of their wily ways and if one of them must be my mother, I need to continue to see how they will prepare the pathway for me.

VICKY

Finally. After all of that. The deed is done. I'll just text
Eliza to let her know. She'll have been wondering about me all
weekend. I can't believe it was so tricky. Booking a romantic
night away in a relaxing spa hotel should have made it easier but
I'm exhausted now.

I can't remember which website I was on when I read that
it's a common anxiety amongst men, that they don't want to have
sex any more when their partner is pregnant, for fear of hurting
the baby or something, but it hasn't half made my job harder. If
only Dan knew quite how ridiculous he was being. I was sure I'd
be able to persuade him otherwise the last couple of weeks but
being his usual stubborn self, there's been no shifting him. Nope,
no bedroom action for us. Fancy having to go to all of this
expense.

Anyway, the hotel's been every bit as wonderful as the
reviews on the website said. And if, according to that ovulation
calendar I used on the internet, I'm ovulating today, then we
couldn't have waited any longer. Getting pregnant next month
would be far too suspicious. Yes, drastic times call for drastic
measures. And hey, hopefully if I keep my legs peddling in the

air, like Eliza told me to, my bun is baking in the oven right now. I'd better stop doing this before Dan gets back from the gym. I'm sure he only went down there so I didn't pounce on him again.

Well, he should have been more obliging yesterday. Seriously, when has he ever come into a hotel room and gone straight down to the gym? Normally, it's shoes off, sit down, quick flick of the television channels while I make a coffee with those sachet things, which is always cold by the time we've tested out the bed. But oh, no. Not this time. He couldn't wriggle out of a 'freebie' night in a hotel that I'd 'won' - I must remember to give Eliza the cash for it when her credit card bill comes through - but when it came to being in any sort of physical contact with me, he turns into bloody Hussain Bolt all of a sudden. Not funny.

He was no better last night either. Our candlelit meal in the hotel restaurant, with that wonderful pianist playing in the corner, certainly put me in the mood. Pity I couldn't have any vino to go with that fabulous steak. Dan made up for it and finished the whole bottle. Why he didn't just order a lager, I'll never know. He says it's not the 'done' thing in places like this but who'd have cared? I'd forgotten how sleepy wine makes him on the rare occasions he drinks it, so I really thought he was joking when we got back to the room and he flopped on the bed, declaring, "I might be asleep when yer done in't bathroom, love."

As predicted, he was snoring like a donkey by the time I'd finished having a wee and brushing my teeth. I stood no chance of waking him. I have to admit, I was starting to panic a bit by this stage.

But it didn't last long. I shouldn't have worried. That's when I realised that if I woke up before him, he wouldn't be able to resist a bit of Morning Glory. I slept well, nestled in this huge, comfy bed, knowing that the alarm was set on my mobile. Once a Girl Guide, always a Girl Guide. Well, the preparation stuff, not the morning sex stuff.

I was a bit worried Dan would wonder why I'd set an alarm on a weekend away but I experienced that strange phenomenon of waking up ten minutes before whatever time the alarm is set, so I was glad I was able to switch it off before he heard a thing.

Dan must have got cold in the night and had managed to undress and climb under the covers next to me. He was lying on his back, still snoring away when I slowly rolled over towards him and stroked his chest, nestling my head into the space between his collar bone and his ribs. The amount of time we must have spent lying like this, over the last few years... It's where I feel safest in the world. Wrapping my especially smoothed left leg over his muscular right thigh, I knew he would rouse when I kissed his neck, then that special spot further towards his ear. His snoring eased into a pleasured snuffle when I move my hand down to see if Mother Nature was on my side.

Sure enough, he was ripe and ready. His expression was rather funny as I straddled his abdomen and began the deed. He was like a little boy who wakes up on Christmas morning and can't quite believe he's not dreaming. It didn't really matter that it lasted no time at all. It felt a bit different to usual, more purposeful. I mean, I'm not saying that I didn't enjoy it and I tried to secure it in my memory as the time our child was conceived. But in a weird kind of way, it was like I was simply collecting something, my crucial ingredient.

When I think about it like that, I do feel a bit guilty. But it's not as if I'm trying to achieve something he's going to be unhappy about. Dan's been delighted about our 'baby' this last couple of weeks. He must have told everyone we know. I loved it when I was the first topic of conversation at the committee meeting the other night. Barbara and Frances were telling me all about which hospital I should use and which antenatal groups were better than others. Old Norman even lent me the cushion he usually brings for his bad back, bless him. There was certainly no mention of the blasted teabags this month. Imagine what things will be like when the baby's actually here. No, in the grand scheme of things, what Dan doesn't know, will never hurt him. He'll never find out, we'll have our perfect little baby to coo over and we'll live happily ever after.

Eliza does keep reminding me that sometimes it takes a while and things don't work out, like when she was trying for her second for a few months. But we're both young and healthy and I can't see any reason why it won't happen for us.

NELL

It's been a surreal couple of weeks. I know I've been watching Ric's every move like a hawk. I feel dreadful that I even checked his text messages the other day. I've always believed that when trust is gone there can be no love left. But the reality is, I do love him, and whatever he's up to with Jeanette, I'm going to fight for him. We've got too much to lose and too much history to throw it all away. But I will find out, in time. For now, I'm concentrating on me and him.

I find myself taking a bit longer to choose what I wear each morning and straightening my hair rather than just scraping it back in a ponytail. I've even had my lipstick on every day. I know it sounds shallow, but Ric wanted me once upon a time and I'm going to make sure he remembers who I was, not just who I am now.

I think he's really enjoyed having dinner together each evening too. I still believe that it's better for Rosie if I eat with her and Ric warms his dinner up when he gets home from work but at the moment, I need him to feel part of our family too.

Last night was so special. Up until then, it was obvious we had been avoiding each other at bedtime, claiming to be desperate to finish a chapter of a book or watch another episode of a programme on television. Ric's clearly getting his fill elsewhere in that department and I just couldn't get the image of him with another woman out of my head. Then last night, finally, my body and mind felt back to normal, whatever that is. I know that the medical advice from the doctors and nurses was to wait a for a whole natural cycle to pass before we start to try again for another baby. But they don't know my body like I do and I just feel ready.

Ric's always a sucker for the Shepherd's Pie I made last night. "You can stick your pizzas an' your pastas," he always says, "'cos there's nothing like an English Shepherd's Pie." Thanks for your special recipe, Mum.

A new set of candles and that CD Ric got me for Christmas, would have made anyone glad to be back from work and as we settled down on the sofa after our meal, I felt closer than we'd been in a long time.

Hours seemed to go by before we'd run out of things to chat about, not about Rosie or the restaurant but about life, like we used to in the old days. We did laugh when we dreamed about the holiday we would like to have this summer and then compared it to the one we can probably afford. And I do love his version of the story of our first date, when Ric pretended he had a car and said that he had to take me home by bus because it was in the garage being repaired.

Luckily, the miscarriage never came up because in a way, it was nice not to think about it for an hour or two. And when Ric silently held my gaze for that extra second, I knew that it was time.

After he held my hand and led me up the stairs, we kissed and touched, like strangers exploring each other's bodies for the very first time. For that moment, I wasn't anyone's mother or wife, I was just me. And Ric, well, he was someone else, someone who made me feel important again. Making love has never felt as special as it did last night. I was a china doll which Ric desired but was afraid to break. What we have lacked in words, recently, we communicated with our bodies and I felt reconnected to Ric once more.

When we lay on the bed and Ric asked me if that had been okay, I couldn't help but hope that a new life had been created in that spark that had ignited between us. I know it sounds silly, but I have a strange feeling that something did happen in my womb last night. I read on the internet about the rise in fertility after a miscarriage and that your chance of having twins is increased.

Now I'm not quite sure how we'd cope with that. But what I am certain of, is that we're back on track and whatever Ric chooses to do outside of our marital bed cannot match what I can give him inside it.

SHANNON

Shit, shit, shitty shit. Where did that go? I swear I 'ad it in my hand when I stood up from the sofa. I must've dropped it on the carpet in there 'cos it's defo not in this bathroom. Let's 'ave a look. Christ this carpet is horrible. I mean who'd put this thing on their floor anyway? I know it's only a caravan but can you imagine lookin' at all the carpets in the shop and decidin', "Yes please, I'll take this one. That's right the one that looks like a scruffy brown dog." An' it smells like one when you get down close to it like this. I wonder if Rhys's mam's ever hoovered in here. There's all sorts of crap trodden into it. Everythin' but my pill.

I knew my plan was goin' too well. Rhys hasn't suspected a thing. My pill packet has stayed on the shelf next to the telly, like the nurse said, so we can both take responsibility for them, an' as long as they disappear on the right day, he's none the wiser whether they've gone down me neck or down the bog.

Sex has been much nicer since we stopped using the condoms. I know the nurse said that we should still use them, just to be doubly sure, but like we said when we got back 'ere, we both know that neither of us 'ave been with anyone else so we're well safe. Rhys can't stand using a condom an' he's right, it does stop the flow of things and feels a bit funny. Now, it's much more natural and I think we're both gettin' better at it.

Bloody 'ell, that nurse at the clinic would 'ave a fit if she knew he'd ditched the condoms an' I was flushin' me pills down the bog. Kind 'o defeats the point o' goin' really. But Rhys's mam would've chucked a bennie if we 'adn't made the appointment. "I can't afford to feed no more little buggers," she said. It was proper embarrassin'.

But at least Rhys came with me. An' the nurse was alright. I liked they way she didn't say we shouldn't be doin' it an' she talked to us like we were grown ups, not kids. She gave us a whole pile of free condoms. I'll give them to Sian at school on Monday. I've actually read those leaflets too, when Rhys has been at work. I know they're meant to tell you 'ow not to get pregnant but from what I can see, if I don't take the pills the nurse prescribed me, an' we do it every day, then we stand a fair chance of me gettin' up the duff.

An' then it's free 'ouse here we come. I can't wait. I wonder what it'll be like. It's gotta be better than this shit 'ole. I've given up lookin' for that pill. The scruffy dog's probably eaten it or somethin'. One thing's for sure, Rhys'll never find it in there.

I think I do actually love Rhys. Sian says you just know when you find the right one. Her mam and dad met at school when they were thirteen and still get off with each other on the sofa when they think no-one's lookin'. Gross. An' I was thinkin' about that this mornin' an' I do just know I love Rhys. I mean, I know our 'ouse isn't perfect yet but I do love livin' with 'im. He makes me laugh all the time an' he shares all his money from work with me. It's well sweet 'ow he brings me a bar of chocolate 'ome every night when he goes for his scratch card an' he makes me guess which one it is. I've only got the *KitKat* right so far.

An' if I am goin' to 'ave a baby with someone, then I can't think of anyone I'd rather 'ave one with, not even Evan Jones. Rhys is proper nice to his little brothers and sisters so I think he'd be good with his own. I mean, I'm guessin' he wouldn't want his own yet, out of choice, an' that's why I can't tell 'im what I'm up to. But if it were to just 'appen ... Well, I think he'd be well excited.

Maybe it already has 'appened. I could be sitting here preggers now. Now there's a thought. It'd be wonderful, really.

Whether Rhys sticks around or buggers off like ginger Chantelle's boyfriend, I know I'll love my baby. Even if I've got no money and can never go out anywhere, I'll be the best mam I can. I'll feed my baby and bath him or her every night and change their pyjamas all the time. I'll always have time to play and never say I'm too busy. I'll listen to them too. Not like hear what they're saying while I'm watchin' telly but really listen and try to help with whatever they're worried about. I will try to get a job eventually and work hard to make sure my child has what they need. And no man will ever be more important to me. My child will always come first and I'll always take their side over anyone else's.

SARAH

I'm so tired and yet I can't sleep. Usually, listening to Tim's choice of radio station and their 'discussion topic' is more than enough to send me off to the Land of Nod when he's driving us somewhere, but not today. My body aches for my bed and that's where I'll be headed as soon as we get home but right now, my mind is whirring to say the least.

Never in a million years did I think this whole process would happen so quickly. I imagined we'd have appointment after appointment and months of waiting lists in between. It's amazing what they can do when money is involved. No-one at work would believe that they had an initial meeting with us only two days after I rang the fertility clinic. How different it all is to my hospital.

It's a good job Tim didn't need any persuasion, really. Poor thing looked so hungover when he got back from his stag do that weekend but he lit up when I mentioned that I'd been doing some reconsidering. "That's exactly what I've been thinking!" I remember he beamed. I'm sure he'd agree with me if I said the sky was green and the grass was blue, sometimes. He's like a little puppy, so eager to please and do the right thing. I do find myself wondering what he really feels and thinks. But surely he wouldn't just be saying what I wanted to hear about something as monumentally important as this.

When I explained that I didn't want to go down the long, laborious route that we'd been pursuing before, he did point out that it was sensible to just pay for some IVF right away if that's where we were going to end up anyway.

After lots of research, the clinic I finally chose almost bent over backwards, to get the ball rolling. A doctor's referral wasn't necessary in this case, they said. Thank God we had to book our individual medical examinations on different days as our shifts were both funny that week. So it wasn't even difficult telling them about my previous pregnancy and asking them to keep it confidential. Tim was ten foot tall when he came home with the news that he had a clean bill of health and some Chinese food to celebrate.

In fact, it's all been almost too good to be true: the ovulation prevention drugs were fine, the baseline ultrasound showed exactly what it ought to and my ovaries were stimulated after only about a week. As I had the trigger shot the other day, I kept thinking of Ellie. I mean, I know that selfishly, I might get my baby out of all of this, and I cannot thank her enough for that.

Without her youthful optimism that anything is truly possible when you put your mind to it, Tim and I would never have come this far. But more than that, I feel like for the first time in her short life, I am her mother. She needs me and I am trying to help her. And there's no feeling as wonderful as that. Even through the discomfort of the egg retrieval today, I focused on her pain and what she has already been through, never mind what she may have to come. That part doesn't even bear thinking about.

Of course, Tim still has no idea about Ellie. I know he is an easy going man and would understand my past. But there's just never been an appropriate moment to tell him about it all before and I don't think now is the right time. What if he didn't agree with the ethics of donor babies? This could be the one time he doesn't simply let me have my own way. Time is of the essence for Ellie and I can't afford any hesitations. No, this whole can of worms is not to be opened yet. It can wait. The way I justify in my head, we could easily be going through this process for ourselves. Ellie has just been a Guardian Angel pointing us in the right direction. In time, when things have settled down, and if we're lucky enough to have a successful pregnancy, I'll introduce him to Ellie and I'm sure that I can talk him round to the idea once he meets her.

For now, I'm taking each day at a time and enjoying my run of good fortune. I pray that it will continue and as we're driving home, Tim's little swimmers are fighting their way through the wall of my microscopic egg. It's not a very romantic start to life, I know, but I don't remember anything very romantic about my adolescent fumblings the first time I conceived. In the grand scheme of things, that bit just doesn't seem so important any more. Tim and I have the rest of our lives to be romantic together. All I hope is that, with God's grace, an embryo is developing in that laboratory, a miracle that will not only create life but breathe life into my first born child.

ME

As my ethereal state is clearly ending and I am about to become substance once more, I'm beginning to see why each of these women could, one day, deliver my soul back to Earth. If I gaze beyond the deceit, I suppose I am beginning to see that they are all determined people who will fight for what they believe in their hearts. Who can deny that this is an admirable trait? They are not harming or hurting anyone, just trying to make the best of their lot. Not one of them sees the obstacles in the way of their goal and I truly believe that they intend to be good people. That quality will be useful to guide me in the greatness I feel my future holds. Each of them has their imperfections, as I did each time I was Human, and I cannot condone their lies, but I do admire their fortitude and their resilience. In addition to this, I can now see that I will live in a land of vast opportunity, with a mother who, to varying degrees, will enable me to access such advantages. She will love me, protect me and fight for me, allowing me to be a child and experience even more privilege than she herself has known.

But time is running out though. In a matter of days, one of these women will have undergone the miracle of conception.

Each of them has set the scene for my new story to begin but that very performance, by which we were all created, is an epic tale in itself. Of the three hundred million players sent on stage by the male, very few will survive to the last act. The challenges they must encounter and defeat make it a true marvel that any of them could greet the damsel in the finale. It is true that every Human Being has endured their toughest test of character before they even take recognisable form. And all of this presumes that the script writers time the last scenes to perfection. If the damsel is not ready or has already exited the stage, then there can be no conclusion. The miracle continues as the actors must deliver the exact words to one another so that the information they carry can be shared as they take that last waltz across the stage and enjoy their happily ever after. It is hard to believe that my new life will have faced and overcome these incredible physical odds before it can encompass my soul.

As if Nature's party trick wasn't awesome enough, my mother will have to carry and nurture my body within her own for over nine months. I will be a parasite, greedily taking what I need to grow and she won't mind at all, taking great delight in bearing the burden of another she has not yet even met. Her physical agony will bring forth joy as I take my first lung full of air and she won't begrudge a single second of the toll I have taken on her exhausted frame.

And so our relationship will continue. I will demand and she will give. She will teach me all she knows and divert me from dangers I will encounter. She would lay down her life for me, given the chance, and love me no matter what.

Just as I thought my future was finally eclipsing my reveries, I am recalling that I have lived this powerful relationship between mother and child before. I must let it flow and remember, for there may be something more to be learned.

KLARA

This existence is the most disturbing so far. Blurred sensations just beg to be untangled. I see no images yet but feel love of the most overwhelming kind, love for a child growing inside me. I have wanted this so much and am savouring every day that I carry around my swollen abdomen. I feel my child moving and stretching in her limited space and I smile each time she hiccoughs.

But I also feel hatred. Hatred for the man who gave her to me but will take her from me soon. I remember that once, I felt something for him, when he showed me kindness and then gratitude for what he had done. But never love. And certainly not now, since things have changed.

Wrestling inside of me are feelings of envy that I have for the poor women that he employs. Despite their ten hour days in the factory, their hunger and their disappointment that really, life in the city is not so very different to that which they had on the farms, I admit that I am jealous.

It's all coming back to me now. Each morning as they gingerly pass my window on their way to the spindles and the looms, I look down as they walk across the courtyard and hear them laughing about the life their parents promised them when their families became emancipated from serfdom. I cannot help but agree that they are very unfortunate indeed and then I pray that the Tsar will soon see how much reform is actually needed in our vast and suffering land. But when they finish their day, and return to the dormitories my husband has provided for married couples, oh how I wish I could trade places with any one of them.

These lucky ones go home to someone who loves and cherishes them. Someone who speaks to them in a civil tongue and doesn't come back each evening with a belly full of vodka. That would be more valuable than any cotton mill owner.

I remember the day my parents introduced me to this portly gentleman who had travelled all the way from Moscow. I thought he must be a friend of my father's, considering his age and appearance. But it was not my father, or my mother, or my sisters he was interested in over dinner. It was me. He asked what I wanted to do with my life and when I told him I wanted to study and to read medicine, he laughed and told me he could take me past the University in his city one day if I went to visit him. My naivety told me that this was an opportunity and I answered all of his questions with eager anticipation that he might fulfil his promise.

Over the next few months, Shapiro visited frequently and then one day I was told that I was to go and live with him as his wife. Too young and inexperienced to disagree with my parents, I went. Never before had I considered marriage or husbands and as the eldest child, had no knowledge of how this arrangement would be made for me. It seemed like an adventure going to the city and as this kind gentleman drove his carriage into Moscow, I'm sure I caught a glimpse of the University. But my days of cooking and cleaning taught me nothing of medicine. I wanted for nothing though and Shapiro showered me with gifts, treating me like nobility rather than a mere farmer's daughter. For this I was grateful and tried to love him in return.

But after only a few short weeks, I became acquainted with the real Shapiro Ivanov. Every evening, I could predict his return from his revelries; a loud thud would alert me that his massive body had shaken the door frame once again. As he bounded in and tried to regain his balance, I would scurry around making sure that supper was ready quickly, for the sooner he ate, the sooner he would go upstairs, fall asleep and my peaceful evening would resume.

Things got worse the evening that I attempted to make borscht. I'd watched my mother make it so many times and was convinced that mine tasted every bit as good as hers. But Shapiro clearly did not agree. He took one sip and threw it across the room. The blood-like stains ran down the walls, warning me of my fate.

Of course he was remorseful the next morning and he sent one of the factory girls to the door of our house to deliver a pair of the softest leather gloves I had ever seen. And I forgave him. Without vodka, he could be such a kind and loving man.

But it seemed that this flash of his true soul had opened the floodgates for further revelations of character. Less than a week later, he deemed the house unclean and asked what I had been doing with my day. As my mouth opened to explain, it was met with a meaty fist and this time the blood splatter was real.

When the inn he frequented was closed for two days, I was more than relieved. The old Shapiro returned and for those couple of evenings, I learned how it could have been to be happily married. We ate dinner together and he talked to me and asked me questions, like he had done on my parents' farm. It was then that he talked about having a family of our own, a son to take over the mill when his days were over. Having only ever been party to the conjugal rights he had exercised on the night of our wedding, I let him teach me more and we became closer physically and perhaps emotionally over the next few days.

It wasn't long before I noticed changes in my body and realised that Shapiro's son and heir was on his way. The prospect excited me more than I ever knew was possible. Having helped mother to look after my younger siblings, I knew of the hard work and sleepless nights ahead but I could not wait for my baby to arrive. I would have someone to share my days with, someone to teach and someone to adore. No longer would I be lonely or search for chores to fill my time. This new person wouldn't judge me or hurt me but love me like I loved them.

It also occurred to me that Shapiro might change with the weighty responsibility of parenthood. Surely he wouldn't want to spend every evening drinking with the other factory owners when he could be at home with us and without the vodka, I would no longer have to dodge his fists.

But no, this was far too optimistic. Nothing changed at all. My life was to irreparably alter, the night I told my husband of my dream. For almost a week, a dream had come to me of the daughter we were to receive. A small girl, with curly brown hair sat on my lap and together we sang until she fell asleep in my arms. She was so beautiful and so real that one night, before we went to sleep, I had to tell Shapiro of my vision, convinced that I'd seen into the future.

I thought this would warm his heart but I was wrong. His loud bellowing voice demanded that I stopped talking such nonsense. Didn't I know that wishing for a girl would create a girl, when it was a son he needed to look after the factory at the end of his days? His booming voice rings clear in my mind even now, and he stood up, towering over me as I rested by the fire. Afraid of what might happen if he pushed me backwards in to the flames, I stood up and headed towards the other room. Shapiro took this as a sign I was not paying attention to his point and followed me. The moment he grabbed my shoulder to drag me back was the exact point at which I passed the top of the stairs. I'm not sure whether it was the shock of the whole episode or my increasing size which knocked my balance, but I lost my footing.

Time slowed down and I realised there was no substance beneath my body. As I tumbled down the stairs and my body was no longer in my control, I shouted for Shapiro. Lying at the bottom, unable to move any of my limbs, I saw him standing, motionless, frozen to the top step. Eventually he came down to help me but I knew what had happened already. I regained movement in my arms and legs and was able to sit upright but I glanced down and saw the blood flowing from my thighs. It was this, rather than the excruciating pain in my back, which made me cry. I knew my baby had been taken.

The rest of that night is unclear. I believe the mind has a way of erasing that which is truly unbearable. I know that a lady from the factory was brought over to deliver my tiny, silent child and I know that I slept for a very long time. But beyond that I see only black.

Maybe I died too that night. Or maybe I survived for a while and joined Shapiro in the annihilation that the life of an alcoholic can bring. But what I do know is that part of my soul fled with that child and as she greeted me at the end of my days as Klara, we sang those songs together once more.

ME

How did this not occur to me before now? All of this time I have focused on my future mother, but in doing so, I have ignored the men who may become my father. Yes, I know who they may be but I have paid little attention to the role they would play in my future.

As Shapiro taught me, when I was Klara, it takes two people to shape the life of a child. Perhaps he would have changed and been a good father but such alterations in Human Nature are rare and I suspect he would have continued to make me, and as such my child, utterly miserable. Of course, a child can survive without the influence of a decent man, but how much more enriched can they be with the emotional stability of a positive male role model? And equally, how much damage can be done by an inadequate one?

As my delivery draws ever closer, I am compelled to visit the men who might be my father and discover how they could help me grow. I don't have enough strength left in my wandering soul to step inside their minds, but I can watch and learn, nonetheless.

DAN

"Cheers, love," Dan thanks a blonde lady who places two pints of lager on the wooden bar which divides them. She takes his bank note and returns some coins. Pocketing the change, he sits at a stool, sipping from one of the drinks. A troubled expression swims over Dan's face. I sense that his thoughts are far away.

His mind returns to the warmth of his surroundings when the recipient of the second drink arrives. "'ow do, fella?" he politely enquires and slides the glass along to the next bar stool.

John takes off his coat and accepts the invitation, explaining that he's "grand" because he will be staying here for tonight's football match, "'cos I've got rid o' satellite. It were too much bloody money."

"Wish Vicky'd let me get rid o' ours but she'd never 'ear of it, not that she watches owt on it, like, but she'd never have the dish taken down. 'Tis too expensive, yer right. An' we could do wi' all extra money now, what wi' weddin' 'n' baby 'n' all that."

"Aye, 'ow's all that goin'?"

"Oh, y'know, she's got it all taken care of. Just gives me bills," Dan laughs off.

"You alright wi' it all though fella?"

"I never knew y' cared!" Dan jokingly puts his arm around his drinking partner and draws him nearer in a show of mock affection, which aims to hide the awkwardness of being asked about his emotions.

"Y'know what I mean," John is clearly trying his best to show concern for his friend, despite Dan's attempts to retain their usual level of witty repartee.

"Yes, I suppose I am, mate," Dan concedes, "Vicky has always been the one for me, you know that. From the moment she served me a pint, on this very spot, I knew she'd be mine forever. I know you'll laugh at that an' say I'm a right soft bugger, but it's true. I'd never been so keen to get the next round in, as I was when she was the new barmaid!"

"Aye, we did notice!" John recalls.

"An' when she said she'd come out wi' me, I couldn't believe me luck. We 'ad such a laugh. An' we still do. An' she's right hardworkin' like, y'know, wants a nice life for us both. An' she still makes the effort with 'erself, y'know?" he winks.

"Alright mate," John frowns in mock disgust, "I get the picture."

"Sorry, it's just the last few weeks have 'ad me head spinnin'. All I'm tryin' to say is that I'm thrilled about the baby an' gettin' married an' all. But, well, I don't think I've been as enthusiastic about it as Vicky'd like me to be. It's just that, well," Dan lowers his voice further so that John is his only confidante, "You'll understand that I'm worried it's all too good t'be true. I just keep remindin' meself that Vicky's different to Carrie an' it's not goin' to 'appen again."

"That's what I were meanin' y'daft bastard," John's caring attitude is nearing its limit but it is clear that Dan has been waiting for someone with whom to share his worries and his monologue has only just begun.

"I jus' couldn't bear it if that 'appened again. T'be left there standin' in front of all me family an' friends, like a dick, wi' everyone all dressed up an' no bride turnin' up."

"No-one thought you were a dick, mate, we all just felt sorry for you. Does Vicky even know about any o' that?"

"Nah, never seemed the thing to talk about. She doesn't really talk about exes, so I don't neither. I mean me folks've mentioned Carrie once o' twice when she's been there but nothin' so as she'd think it was anythin' other than just an' old girlfriend."

"An' I s'ppose she doesn't know that many of the folk 'round 'ere that would remember, eh?"

"S'ppose. But I'll probably have t'tell 'er sometime soon if were goin' have a child together, y'know. She's got a right t' know. I'd want to know. But not now, not while she's on a high about it all," Dan mulls over his thoughts.

"D'y'ever 'ear owt from Carrie?" John tentatively asks, while ordering two more pints of lager.

"Y'must be fuckin' jokin'" comes the reply.

"I jus' thought, y'know," this time it is John's voice which lowers, "she might've been after y' for money o' somethin' for the little 'un."

"Nah, not even."

And now I understand. There is a silence. It's not an awkward silence but a comfortable one, between two people who know each other well enough to pause and take a rest from their conversation before it will inevitably resume in a moment or two.

"No, not a sniff of 'er shit since that text from 'er sister that told me she thought I had the right to know she'd 'ad a baby."

Again, there is time for digestion of this information as the two men continue to drain their second drink.

"So it was definitely yours then?" John probes further, "I mean, y'don't 'ave to tell me owt but well, I've never 'eard y'talk about it before now so I didn't like to ask."

"I try not to think about it mate, t'be honest, but this last few weeks's just brought it all back, y'know."

"Aye, I'll bet it 'as," John sympathises.

"'er sister told me it were mine but 'ow would I ever know? It could o' been but then as you well know, she were shaggin' 'alf o'Freddock by all accounts."

"Don't know about that, Dannyboy, but that pillock from Freddock Butchers were the one ev'ryone were talkin' about. Bloody good job she's never set foot back in t'village, really. Plenty o' the lasses would be ready for words with 'er."

"True. But that didn't make my life any easier, did it? I never got to know where she went when she got found out. I mean, gettin' jilted at the altar's bad enough but not knowin' where she was t' get an explanantion ... an' then findin' out she might've been 'avin yer kid ...an' 'avin' to wonder about it for four years ... I don't know if I've got a son or a daughter or nothin' belongin' to me out there ... an' well, that's enough to fuck up anyone, t'be honest," Dan exhales deeply after his outpourings and lets go of the air it has taken to complete his lengthy sentence as well as the anguish he has been carrying for so long.

"Well," John finally contributes, "lighnin' don't strike twice, mate, an' as y'say, Vicky's not like that. You've got to move on an' jus' let this one make y'happy."

"Yer right, I have. I've been 'alf waitin' for summit t'go wrong but it's not goin' to, is it? This time we're goin' to 'ave the best weddin' I can afford an' I'm goin' t'be the Dad I've not been allowed to be for all these years." There is a long pause before Dan catches the bar tender's eye and with the first true smile I've seen from him, he requests, "Another couple o'pints please, love."

RIC

"Don't take this the wrong way, Ric but why d'you want me to come to the wholesaler's with you? You always go yourself." Jeanette asks as she opens the rusty passenger door of Ric's once-white Caddy van.

"I, er, just thought you might want to learn a few more, how you say? Facets of the business," comes the response. "I can leave you to clean the tables again if you like? Come on, they sell coffee." I dread the confirmation of Nell's suspicions as I see these two alone together.

Driving along, discussing the items they will need to purchase for the restaurant, there is little of the insight I need into this man and his relationship with the young waitress.

Finally, Jeanette asks, "So how's your wife doing?"

"So so," Ric shrugs as he changes gear. "My Nelly, she always tries to put a brave face on, you know? So she seem fine to everyone but only I know the truth when I look in her eyes. An' even then, she not always tell me all of how she feels."

"That must be difficult to cope with then," Jeanette says while texting on her phone.

"Yeah, but she had a really tough time, you know. She's a good Mama an' all she wants is to have lots of bambinos to run aroun' the house," Ric explains. "When she lost the baby, she hurt so much, you know. An' I'm not so good with these things. I never say the right words. It would have been better if she had her own Mama to talk to but she not with us anymore. It so sad watching the one you love aching inside, when there's nothing you can do to take that pain away," Ric beats his chest emphatically to express his last point.

"Yeah, I know," Jeanette agrees thoughtfully and pauses messaging on her phone.

"So anyway," Ric lightens his tone, "your Dad still looking for a business to buy for you?"

"Yeah, something like that. I mean I've got to finish my degree first but, all going well, he says it's the sensible solution. There are so few graduate jobs out there and he's got some cash to invest so we figure I might as well put 'Business Management' into practice."

"You'd be good in the restaurant trade," Ric hints but is interrupted by a shrill ringing from Jeanette's phone.

After only a few moments, the conversation ends and Jeanette looks blankly at her handset.

"You lost signal? The reception's shit out here," Ric tells her, "Was that Amy?"

"Yep. Probably a good thing we got cut off. She was screaming at me to stop texting her."

"I though you two would have sorted things out by now. It's weeks since you had that bust up," Ric pulls up into the car park but no-one gets out as Jeanette begins to weep.

"It's just such a mess, Ric. It's no better than it was last time I talked to you about it. She doesn't trust me and thinks that every time I go out clubbing without her, I'm snogging someone else."

"Well, you know what I think?" Ric offers, "I think that she not good for you. She suffocate you. But, if you love her and want to be together, then I think you are too young to be living together. Move out. Find another student house. It would be much healthier. You gonna end up like an' old married couple before you're twenty one!"

"Easier said than done though. The rent on our house is pretty much the cheapest around so I'd have to ask Mum and Dad for more money for another place, which would mean explaining why and ..." Jeanette trails off.

"Ah," Ric guesses, "They don't know you're gay?"

"Exactly."

"Maybe you should tell them, Jeanette. Would it be so awful? Maybe they would surprise you. Lots of gay people say their families were jus' waiting for them to say something because they already guessed."

"You've got to be kidding! They'd freak out completely. Dad would never be able to look me in the eye again and Mum, well, she'd pretend it was okay but I know it wouldn't be. It's not the sort of thing they would be able to boast about when they go down to the Golf Club and compare notes with other couples about whose kid's doing which degree at which Uni, blah, blah, blah," she mocks.

"I bet they'd come 'round eventually. Being a parent means loving your kid whatever they tell you. You don't always have to agree with them, or their choices, but the love bit, well, it overrides everything. I would love my Rosie whether she straight or a poof."

"You can't say *poof*," Jeanette laughs but as usual, Ric is blindly unaware of his inappropriate terminology.

"What?" he mocks injury.

"Nothing. I just wish I could talk to them the way I can talk to you. I'll always be grateful for the night you let me stay at your house. I was so embarrassed getting upset at work like that. It didn't help that the restaurant was full of couples in love. I'm not sure what I would have done if you hadn't insisted on driving me home. And then when I told you I couldn't face going into the house and you offered to take me to yours, your spare room bed was so nice and cosy. Just having some time away made it all bearable again in the morning."

"Well, you women are all pretty much similar creatures, eh? So I thought, what does Nelly do when she's feeling shit? Puts those bloody smelly candles on, has a good old English cup o' tea, a hot bath and goes to bed. Works every time for her."

"Well, it did work. I just felt awful when you checked your phone to see where your wife and daughter were and realised that your poor wife was in hospital and you were looking after me not her."

"I know. I'm such an idiot sometimes. I lose track of the time. I can't believe I didn't get a speeding ticket on my way to the hospital that night."

Jeanette smiles. "I will sort it out with Amy. One way or another. I can't go on like this, that's for sure. My relationship with her is dominating everything and I can't let it ruin my chances of a good degree. I'll have no chance of getting Dad to buy me a business then if I'm gay and degree-less!"

Ric finally opens the door and Jeanette takes his lead. "Ready for Pasta Buying Lesson One?"

RHYS

"And how's college going on a Wednesday son?" Rhys's boss asks him as he lowers the bonnet of a long, grey estate car.

"Dead good actually," comes the reply as Rhys wheels himself out from underneath the vehicle. "I mean, I always thought that it would be borin' but it's quite interestin'. The tutor wants to sign me up for a business course on a Thursday night 'cos I got some 'alf decent GCSEs, y'know, so he thinks I can manage it as well as the NVQ. Says it would come in 'andy if I ever 'ad me own business, like. But I don't know about that."

"You should go for it, lad. You can never have too many qualifications. You're a bright lad and I'm really pleased how quickly you've picked things up here. As I keep telling you, it'll not be long before I'm happy to leave you here to hold the fort while I have a few days off and that."

Rhys fights a smile at this compliment and darts back under the car. The two continue these infrequent interjections but mostly, the garage is filled with the tinny sound of the radio, as they diagnose and treat each of the motor-patients in their care.

Finally the clock reads five and Rhys is up and wiping his hands on an already grease-sodden rag. "Okay to get off now Bill?" he checks.

"Yes son, see you tomorrow."

Permission granted, Rhys leaves the garage and walks out into the cold, Spring afternoon. It's not long before his phone rings. It is clear from this end of the dialogue that Rhys is being teased by a friend, "I'm not under the thumb. I jus' don't wanna come out tonight that's all," he explains. "I was out last night an' loads of times last week, if you weren't so pissed you'd remember."

There is a pause while Rhys's friend must be heightening the persuasion.

"Listen," Rhys continues, "I've got a fit bird to go 'ome to. Why would I want to be goin' out all the time? Who wants to go out for *MacDonalds* when they got steak at home?" With that the conversation ends.

Rhys puts his phone back in his pocket as he enters the newsagents. At the confectionary counter, he swiftly picks up a *Mars Bar* but then stands and deliberates for at least a minute before adding a *Toffee Crisp* to his purchase. With a five pound note, Rhys pays for the chocolate and asks the vendor for a scratch card.

Outside, Rhys hides one chocolate bar in the security of his pocket. The other is unwrapped and quickly eaten. He uses a shiny two pence piece to rub the silver foil coating from the scratch card and blows away the debris before wiping the smooth card with the sleeve of his overall. Pausing at a public litter bin, in anticipation of the inevitable futility of this gamble, Rhys brings the scratch card towards his face for closer inspection. With a look of complete disbelief, he scratches off the peripheral silver foil which he had previously deemed unnecessary and repeatedly rubs the card with his sleeve.

Realisation sets in that his eyes are not deceiving him, and Rhys's jaw drops but no sound comes out. Frozen to the spot, Rhys takes out his mobile phone but then reconsiders, replaces it and runs all the way home, his unburied treasure clasped in his hand.

Perspiring and out of breath, Rhys hammers on the door of the caravan. "It's not locked you daft bugger," a voice yells but he continues to knock, unable to muster the energy to do any more.

The door opens and Rhys falls into the caravan.

"*Flake.* It's a *Flake*, 'cos you just flaked out on the floor, get it? I'm right aren't I?" Shannon looks smug.

Unable to verbally confirm or deny, Rhys holds up the *Toffee Crisp* as well as the winning ticket.

Finally, he manages, "We've only won on the bloody scratch card!"

"'ow much? Will it do our tea?"

"A bit more than that, Shannon. More like it'll do our tea for the next twenty years!"

She replies with only a shriek and the two squeeze each other in an embrace.

When it ends and Rhys's heartbeat and voice return to normal, he looks Shannon in the eye and continues his previous train of thought, "That's if you'll 'ave me for the next twenty years?"

TIM

Like many of the adults on this pretty, suburban cul-de-sac, Tim is pulling onto his driveway at the end of a long day. Mums open car doors for noisy children and Dads quickly swap their suits for sporty gear, keen to squeeze in a pre-dinner run before bath time. But Tim simply carries his lap top bag into the house, and slouches on the sofa. He makes his tie slack around his neck and flicks through his options using the television remote.

No sooner has he settled down to his choice than the door bell rings. He pauses his programme and goes to answer. Standing there is Ellie, shivering.

"Er, hello," Tim is polite but puzzled, "Can I help?"

"I'm erm, a friend of Sarah's," she tests.

"She's at work. Can I tell her who called?"

"It's Ellie. I was just passing and wondered how she's getting on, y'know, with the IVF. How's it going?"

Tim is clearly taken aback by this and invites Ellie to come in from the cold. He shuts the door and they stand in the passageway.

"Sorry if I seem a bit dazed, we'd just agreed not to talk about it to anyone else and so I wasn't expecting you to ask.

Have we met before?" Tim's eyes narrow as he struggles with his memory. He is truly thrown by this encounter.

"Look," Ellie is frank, "I'm Sarah's daughter. She'll go mad at me for telling you but you're going to have to find out sooner or later. And you're hardly going to believe that she's got a 'friend' my age that you've never met before."

Tim is silent.

Ellie eventually fills the gap, "I really am sorry to spring it on you like this. I should have called her before I arrived but I totally forgot what time she works on a Friday."

"It's okay. Come in and have a seat," Tim processes and accepts this life changing revelation and leads the way back to the comfort of the sofa.

"We've only been in contact for a few weeks. I made enquiries about her at the agency, once I turned eighteen. You knew she had a daughter though right?"

"No, actually," Tim admits, "No I didn't."

This time the silence is unfilled and Ellie is out of her depth as Tim gazes out of the window, blinded by this new information.

Ellie glances around the now familiar lounge and pauses at a silver framed photograph of a thinner looking Tim and his young bride.

"So how long have you two been married?" Ellie attempts to infiltrate.

"Ten years this Summer," Tim says without looking from the window. "But we've been together a lot longer," his stock response continues.

"Really?" this time Ellie is genuinely interested.

"Yes," Tim looks to Ellie, "We've been together for seventeen years. Nineteen, if you count the bit at school before she dumped me for a year. You didn't think I was old enough, did you? My youthful good looks give nothing away ..." Tim's attempt at easing the situation with humour is swept away by the possibility that is dawning on the pair.

The realisation that these two could be linked by more than their relationship with Sarah is evident when Tim continues, "Yeah, childhood sweethearts, you might say. She was my first love and I was hers. Never had another girlfriend in the time that we were apart. I didn't see Sarah much that year - we went to a huge school and kept out of each other's way and she was off sick a lot - but I couldn't stop thinking about her and eventually pestered her enough to come to the cinema with me. The rest, as they say, is history. We kind of just picked up where we'd left off."

A knowing look passes between the two but no words are spoken.

"You don't think ... I mean, I just presumed that Sarah would have mentioned if ... Do you reckon ..."

"I do," is all that Tim can reply and his stunned expression gives way to a grin which reaches from ear to ear. "I think I must be ..." The grin has not faded at all and although he avoids the actual words, both know what he means.

"Bloody Hell!" he finally concludes, the grin holding fast.

ME

Well, I am both surprised and thrilled by all of my potential fathers. The doubts I may have held about their suitability from viewing them through my mothers' eyes are truly dispersed by seeing that they are all honest, loyal and of sound moral compass. What more could a child need than to be raised by a man who would provide and care like these men will? But does this knowledge make me gravitate towards one particular pair? I'm not sure that it does. Where I now feel pulled is into the future. I am not yet at my imminent birth. No, the cells are still not united and so my soul awaits attachment to the physical world. This flash forward is to my future and the person I now know I will become.

I see the proud parents bringing their new baby out of the hospital. They walk gingerly from the doorway of the huge building into the brightness of the low November sun, unaware of the leaves sweeping around their ankles or the wind whipping their cheeks. The well-wrapped pink parcel, snuggled in the car seat balancing on her mother's arm, is their sole focus now as the father puts a grey suitcase into the boot of a car and they begin their slow journey home, terrified that anything should disturb or harm their precious cargo. As they arrive home, the little family is greeted by balloons and banners announcing the new arrival to the world. They take their daughter into the warmth of the house and unwrap their gift, her small limbs unfolding as they become free. She cries and they tend. Nature has programmed the two to fulfil every need of the dependent one as she lies, helpless and vulnerable, absorbing every particle of love they feel in their hearts.

I see the toddler playing with her sister. She is a happy child, only just steady on her feet. While Mother folds the clean clothes and sings her favourite nursery rhyme, the tot opens a plastic case containing vibrantly coloured imitations of medical implements. She experiments tentatively on her sibling, looking at her ears through the blood red otoscope and checking her heart still beats with the mustard yellow stethoscope. Her sister complies and remains silent but Mum distracts from potential heavy handedness by reminding the youngster that Dad will be home from work any second and she resumes her place at the window, watching and waiting for her hero to return.

I see the child, running around in the sunshine and laughter of the school playground. The other girls all vie for her attention, offering skipping ropes and suggestions for new games. But the child they compete for is more interested in the little boy sitting on the step, watching them. She goes to him, knowing even in her young years that he is different and yearns, but knows not how, to be involved in their play. He has long since given up trying to infiltrate the boisterous pushing and shoving of the boys in the class. She bends down to his level and tells him which part he will take in the game. He smiles and communicates a noise that the girl has learned to identify as signifying happiness, although his eyes remain fixed on the ground. Together they return to the group and she announces that this is her friend and he will be the elf who visits their fairy kingdom.

I see the girl taking her cat to see the Vet in a plastic ventilated box that is far too big for her to carry but despite her father's offers, she insists on taking Tiger into the building herself. As Dad opens the door, she looks around to catch a glimpse of which other four-legged patients she might be lucky enough to see. When the Vet calls their name, she is quick to explain the problem and lifts her pet out of his box with expert care, which soothes and calms the creature in this alien environment. In one swift pull, a large tick is removed from the cat's head and the girl looks as relieved as the animal. Once she knows he is safely back in his box, it is obvious that the girl is equally as interested in the tick. The Vet takes time to show and explain the parasite's anatomy, clearly identifying a kindred spirit in the girl.

I see the teenager, slim and beautiful yet plain, still resistant to society's pressure to mask these years with the unimportance of designer clothes and cosmetics. She sits in her bedroom surrounded by books, paper and pens. Her eyes eagerly watch a screen which displays the words her fingers are creating on a keyboard. She knows exactly what she must do to complete this Biology assignment for school and gain the highest grade possible. Her mother gently knocks on the door and passes an apple, happy to see her diligence but also concerned that her baby will forget to eat and sleep if she does not remind her.

I see the doctor, fresh faced but confident, waiting for her first patient of her first surgery. She takes a small framed photograph of her parents, snapped on a recent holiday, out of her bag and places it on the desk. Her years of training at the ready, she is more that adequately prepared for the conundrum ahead. An elderly man walks in and quickly, the first of the day's mystery illnesses is solved with a smile. With a glance of silent thanks to her parents, she realises that finally, the dream is coming true.

I see the woman declaring her discovery. It is repeated again and again on every channel on television and broadcast to every country around the world. The news the planet has been waiting for. For decades it has been on its way but she has finally cracked the code and she describes her professional journey with nonchalance in this, now famous, interview. No longer will the Human Race have to live in fear, to think the worst of their body's imperfections and to lose each other to such a terrorist. For this woman has created a serum which will become the birth right of every child. It will protect every cell in the body from hideous mutations. No government will be able to resist its affordability or the pressure from the rest of the World to banish Cancer to history books.

The woman, the doctor, the teenager, the girl, the child, the toddler and the baby rewind at speed and I am left with nothing but peace. I mean real peace. I have no more worries about where my Soul is to be delivered, for I know it will be okay. My next life was always meant to be, just the same as my previous incarnations were set aside for my Soul to experience. This state of calm is not dissimilar to that which I have felt before deaths but it is more, much more intense. I am warm and cool enough, my hunger and thirst are satisfied more than I have ever felt and I feel no need to sleep or wake. This is it. I am ready.

The images in my head, the memories and the knowledge I have recently gained are fading fast. I have seen into a future that I will soon fail to remember until it replays in real time. But I do not care and I can easily discard these thoughts. Like clothes I have outgrown, they are no sooner cast aside than forgotten. I will move on and find my new attire. For I know that where I am headed, I will fulfil my destiny. Fate has consulted with my Soul and loaned it a new body, a new existence and new parents to guide me through her grand plan.

I feel lucky to have been involved in the shortlisting of these special guardians but now there is only one family in my sight. The other three couples will receive the gift of a child, I am sure, when the right spirit seeks them for a home and then they too, will play their part in the enlightenment of the soul of another. For now, I do not see Vicky or Nell or Shannon or Sarah. Earthly shapes lose their form and I just see my Mother. Her name, her age, her wealth and her flaws fade away and I have absolute confidence that she is right for me. She loves me now and forever. She is the only perfection I will ever know. I am drawn close to her and she absorbs me into her very being, wraps me in her instant love and I know I am safe forever. There is nothing more for me to do but wait and grow strong enough to begin my next journey.

This is Helen Bateman's debut novel. She studied English Language and Literature at Lancaster University and has taught both subjects at Secondary school level. She lives in Yorkshire with her husband and looks after their three children full time. Writing is something Helen has always enjoyed and she feels blessed to now have more time to indulge in this privilege.

www.facebook.com/helenbatemanauthor

https://twitter.com/hbatemanauthor

If you like this book please review on Amazon or Goodreads and share with others using #soultotake.

11730198R00119

Printed in Great Britain
by Amazon.co.uk, Ltd.,
Marston Gate.